CASTLES in the Sand
A riveting social drama

Neville Herrington

Copyright

Copyright by Neville Herrington — August 2020©

CASTLES *in the sand*©

The right of *Neville Herrington* to be identified as the author of the work has been asserted in accordance with the Copyright Act 98 of 1978.©

All rights reserved, whether the whole or part of the material is concerned, specifically the rights of translation, reuse of illustrations, recitation, broadcasting, reproduction in other ways, and storage in databanks. No part of this publication may be reproduced or transmitted in electronic, print, web, or other format without the express written permission of the Author.

Published by:
Tekweni Media

Contact
Sandy Herrington
email: sandyh@iafrica.com
web: www.tekweni.co.za

DTP
Clive Thompson
International Professional Book Designer
www.getclive.com
email: cliveleet1@gmail.com
+27 83 761 0698 cell

Printed by
Pinetown Printers, Durban

ISBN: 978-0-620-88611-6

Contents

Chapter 1 .... *9*
Split Loyalties

Chapter 2 .... *20*
A Night Out

Chapter 3 .... *28*
Mr. Blignaut

Chapter 4 .... *35*
A Bad Connection

Chapter 5 .... *44*
Overdose

Chapter 6 .... *50*
On the Warpath

Chapter 7 .... *58*
The Pie Cart

Chapter 8 .... *65*
Hot on The Trail

Chapter 9 .... *76*
Intrigue

Chapter 10 .... *82*
Unexpected Encounter

Chapter 11 .... *91*
Shady Underworld

Chapter 12 .... *103*
MG Sports

Chapter 13 .... *117*
A Date

Chapter 14 .... *124*
A Date with Death

Chapter 15 .... *128*
Finding Love

Chapter 16 .... *133*
Fresh Proposals

Chapter 17 .... *139*
Decisions

Chapter 18 .... *146*
A strange Incident

Chapter 19 .... *151*
Awkward Meeting

Chapter 20 .... *157*
Masks

Chapter 21 .... *161*
Things Fall Apart

Chapter 22 .... *168*
Finger of Suspicion

Chapter 23 .... *174*
The Report

Chapter 24 .... *178*
Getting Away

Chapter 25 .... *183*
The Investigation

Chapter 26 .... *189*
Settling Issues

Chapter 27 .... *198*
New Dimensions

Acknowledgements   213
Other Books by the Author   214

Foreword

As historical fiction **Castles in the Sand** draws the reader into Durban's dangerous sub-culture of the early 1960s. The action peels away the outer layers of respectable middle-class conformity revealing when relationships are based on illusionary expectations, external forces have the potential to destroy the delicate fabric of their imaginary safe worlds, as if it they were no more than fragile sandcastles at the mercy of the incoming tide.

Editor

CASTLES *in the Sand*
A riveting social drama

Neville Herrington

Chapter 1

Split Loyalties

Durban's beachfront was a favourite holiday playground for white South Africans in the early 1960s. The sandy beaches and warm Indian Ocean, candy floss, popcorn, milkshakes, buckets and spades, Punch and Judy shows, rubber surfboards, brightly coloured umbrellas and deck chairs, along with the pungent smell of the salty surf and suntan oil, created a special ambience that left an indelible imprint on many young minds.

It was an enchanted world where young sculptors had free reign in their magic sunny studio to create castles and forts, hoping they would withstand the impact of threatening forces. It was here that dreams were given shape, broken and rebuilt again, until the incoming tide washed them all away… leaving in its wake an early lesson in the transient nature of life.

As the eye drifted down towards the harbour, the heady atmosphere of the holiday ambience of the fun-filled beaches of the popular Golden Mile, began to dissipate as holiday hotels made way for sturdy colonial hospital buildings and residential flats. Directly behind the hospital ran Prince Street with more residential flats, some housing nurses, a doctors' residence, a blood bank and a police station, and running parallel to Prince Street the infamous Point Road with its prostitutes, striptease joints and drugs. For the majority of South Africans at the time, this popular seaside playground was viewed with jaundiced eyes, as it was reserved for the exclusive pleasure of whites, cossetted within a socially-engineered political landscape called apartheid that was vigorously promoted and protected by its chief architect, Dr. Hendrik Verwoerd, who was building a gigantic sandcastle of his own on very shaky foundations. It was in this setting that people played out their daily lives ignoring the media commentators informing them of threatening events that would eventually change the status quo.

As the narrative moves into the early 60s we see wedged between the blood bank and the police station a maisonette where a family drama plays out, showing how external forces have the potential to destroy the delicate fabric of a world built on illusionary expectations, in much the same way as the incoming tide destroys fragile sandcastles on the beach.

It is here that Bessie Cooksley, a widow in her mid-50s, has lived for the past ten years. Her daughter-in-law, Susan Cooksley lives in the other half of the building, and, like a divided building, Susan lives a double life. Her pretty face and slim figure are instant male attractions that she uses as investable physical assets to serve her reckless lifestyle. She is familiar with the streets around the beachfront and finds the posh hotels along the Golden Mile ideal venues to flaunt her vanity as an escort to visiting wealthy businessmen.

Bessie, her mother-in-law, like so many whites at the time, is oblivious to any political undercurrents that are set to culminate in radical changes nearly thirty years later. Her world doesn't extend much beyond the four walls of her modest home with its well-worn décor, as she has kept most of the furniture that she and her late husband had in their cramped house in the gold mining town of Springs, east of Johannesburg. Much of it is cheap kitsch, the result of impulse buying from the OK Bazaars and bargain-basement stores. A gaudy plastic tablecloth covers the dining room table and the famous *Mr. Min* Furniture Polish keeps her ball-and-claw pieces looking spick-and-span, though reeking of fake lavender. A further addition to the atmosphere is a lingering smell of butter-flavoured syrup, indicative of the many Marie biscuits that Bessie consumes, adding to her expanding waistline.

Today she is dressed in a fussy floral frock and pink apron as she prepares to set the supper table by first removing the plastic cover, then carefully spreading out her treasured lacy tablecloth with its geometric embroidered designs. She stubs her cigarette *stompie* and begins to quietly hum the sentimental ballad, *I'll Walk Beside You*, which is interrupted by a knock at the front door.

'Come in. The door's unlocked,' she calls out in a shrill military voice.

Her widowed sister, Winnie, a relief nurse at Addington Hospital who works two days a week, enters and heads straight for the couch to flop down.

'Whew! What a day I've had!'

'Oh, come on, Winnie, every day's a bone-weary one for you.'

'It's just that Reg was home early this evening, drunk as a skunk, and yelling at the top of his voice at all and sundry. When he comes home late it's even worse. Then he's a menace to everyone... including me, as he never switches off the stove, but leaves the plates burning time after time. I told him he could toast the whole building, with me in it.'

'What a disgrace!'

'But tonight, I cooked his meal before I left and instructed him under no circumstances to go into the kitchen.'

Bessie's curlers seem to stand on end when she hears the name, Reg, and is forever thankful for having a good son like George, whom she is expecting to come around for supper. Patting down the curlers on her peroxided hair she continues listening with half an ear to Winnie's prattle when the telephone rings, 'Excuse me, Win.'

Her face drops on hearing the caller's message, and doesn't bother to say goodbye, but drops the receiver as if it were dirt.

'Who was that Bess?'

Bessie moves back to the table and is about to pull the tablecloth off in anger. 'You think you have problems! As usual,

I invited George for supper but he tells me now… at the very last minute… that he and that thing he lives with are going out tonight.'

Wanting to soften the disappointment, Winnie sighs, 'But, I'm here Bess, and only too happy to oblige.'

Bessie returns a dark scowl.

Winnie lights up a cigarette, fatuously asking whether only George was supposed to be coming over.

'Of course not! He would've had to drag that thing along with him…'

'Oh, you mean, Susan?'

'She'd never let him come here alone… not if she could help it. I was also looking forward to seeing little Candice.' Bessie slaps down two large serving spoons on the table before adding in her harsh soprano voice, 'He tells me they're going out to dinner somewhere… and that after all the trouble I took to cook a nice meal.'

Winnie believes that her sister's over-protective attitude towards George is unnatural and amounts to a compulsive personality disorder, but she dares not say anything lest Bessie flies off the handle. So, she offers a half-hearted response. 'Shame, that's not very considerate of them, I know.'

'Considerate, huh! It's not his fault, I know my George, he'd never let his mother down. It's her damn fault. She's behind it, I know. Every Thursday they have dinner here except tonight.'

'Why did they suddenly change their minds?'

Bessie tosses a dirty rag into the sink. 'Ag, it's their bloody wedding anniversary,' her eyes glancing across to a framed photograph on the mantelpiece of George with his arm around his mother, taken before his marriage.

'My Len never forgot our wedding anniversary when he was alive. He always brought me a lovely bunch of flowers,' Winnie reminisces in a sweet tone while Bessie stifles a yawn.

Taking a roast leg of lamb from the oven, Bessie says, 'I feel like throwing this at their front door.'

'How long have they been married for now, Bessie?'

'Who cares! All I know is that the poor man has had to put up with her for much too long... five years... far too long!'

Winnie, who is four years younger than her sister, stands in front of the lounge mirror titivating her appearance, which she believes is more attractive to men than her sister's. She often applies a tone of rouge that makes her cheeks glow like embers. She sits down at the table with her eyes drifting across to a Tretchikoff print of the Chinese Girl hanging on the opposite wall. 'Lovely girl,' she murmurs enviously.

'Who?' snaps Bessie, 'Susan?'

'No, I was admiring your Chinese girl.'

'Oh, that! I bought that at the OK Bazaars.'

'I like her lovely red cheeks against the greenish facial tones ... now that's what I call a pretty woman.'

Bessie, whose mind is locked on her daughter-in-law, replies, 'She's just a jumped-up tart!'

Winnie is affronted that she should say such a nasty thing about the Chinese girl, turns to take another look at the print. Bessie, following her gaze, responds angrily, 'Not her! That thing next door.'

'Oh, yes, I think it's a disgrace the way she treats you... after all, you've done for them.'

'You know, up until two months ago, I used to be taken to the drive-in on a Friday night. But then I heard from her ladyship's maid... yes, from the maid, mind you... that she was sick 'n tired of having to drag the old woman around with them.'

'Really! What a terrible thing to say!'

Winnie is anxious for Bessie to serve dinner as she is feeling peckish and has heard enough of her whinging and fault-findings. But Bessie is not going to let a sympathetic ear be shut so soon, so she sits down opposite Winnie and with a look of utter disgust, says, 'Do I look like an old woman?'

At a loss for words, Winnie looks at the greyish wart on the right side of Bessie's nose.

'Well, speak up, do I?' demands Bessie.

'You're a fine-looking woman for your age, take my word for it.'

Bessie gives an unappreciative grunt and continues with her gripe. 'To be referred to in the servant's quarters as the old woman... now that really gets my goat!'

'You're quite right, Bessie. Not at your age.'

'My age has got nothing to do with it. And just because you're four years younger than me and think you're prettier has not won you any men since Len died.'

Winnie slaps down her serviette, 'You've always been jealous of me, Bessie. Right-back since schooldays, when Jimmy Davis preferred me to you. You can't stand it, can you?'

'I'm not jealous of you... silly old cow! Now stop talking nonsense.'

Placating her sister in anticipation of a good meal, Winnie says soothingly, 'And you do so much for them, Bessie.'

There is no limit to Bessie's self-pity in playing the martyred mother. 'I'm considered good enough to babysit... but not tonight, I said, no siree! I told them straight, if you're not coming here to eat, you can ask the maid to babysit. I mean that woman just takes advantage of me all the time.'

Winnie's mouth is watering as she mentally consumes the glistening baked brown leg of lamb emitting a rich and tempting aroma yet feels obliged to make a suitable reply. 'It's the same all over, Bessie, let me tell you.'

'What do you mean the same? This one's the leader of the pack.'

'Young women today have no respect for anything. Life's too easy for them,' asserts Winnie, accepting a generous slice of roast lamb, and then helping herself to vegetables and gravy

'My poor George, to be saddled with that piece of rubbish!'

'Young women have become spoilt with all this talk of women's liberation… I mean, what a load of hooey! Women can do what they want if they know how. And all the fancy gadgets they have to pleasure themselves with.'

'You mean like vibrators?'

'That too!'

Winnie gives her sister a wry smile and wink, 'That's quite a fancy gadget!'

'This thing's more than a fancy gadget the way she dresses up.

Three days a week I see her all dolled-up with the excuse that she has to make a good impression when she knocks on people's doors collecting information for a marketing research company that she says she's working for. Good impression, my foot! I don't know what the teachers at Candice's school must think of her, I really don't. She never leaves the house with any of the forms that she says she has to fill in for the company and never brings any home. George trusts her too much and says that she earns good money for the work she does.'

Bessie shovels a mouthful of lamb into her mouth, but before it is properly chewed, she continues her spluttering tirade. 'Sometimes she's back home just before George gets in from work with Candice. My poor George! To be seen in public with that thing! Dressed up like a hambone... with all her fancy frills and whatnots!'

Winnie sputters, 'Hambone! Oh, dear Bessie. Fancy that! A hambone!' A spray of chewed roast lamb flies through the air across the table settling on Bessie, who disgustedly flicks them off with the tips of her fingernails.

But poor Winnie can't contain her mirth. 'Hambone! Oh, Bessie, that sounds so funny,' and she continues chuckling away to herself, with Bessie looking increasingly irritated. 'I can see it,' utters Winnie, nearly choking on another piece of chewed lamb as she blurts out, 'Yes, yes, with little paper frills tied around Susan's pretty legs... and then... and then,' she ejaculates, 'Sprinkled with cinnamon and nutmeg.'

Looking at Winnie as if she has lost her mind, Bessie snaps, 'Oh, stop being a silly bitch!' And stares her sister down before adding, 'Stop giggling like a silly schoolgirl when I want to be serious.'

As Winnie is hoping to be offered a second helping she immediately assumes an attentive demeanour, and utters a nasty comment that Bessie instantly appreciates. 'Sorry Bessie, Susan's just a nasty old pig bone... yes, a smelly pig bone without any cinnamon and nutmeg,' and suppresses a giggle before checking for a response, but none is forthcoming. Winnie then voraciously attacks the next mouthful as if wanting to devour the last remaining piece of Susan's nutmeg and cinnamon leg. In so doing, she can't suppress her mirth a second longer and begins snorting and sniggering all over again before bursting into convulsive laughter, sending tiny spattered pieces of chewed lamb flying across the table. Bessie furiously wipes her face before standing up to declare, 'If you can't conduct a decent conversation, I'm turning on the radio... and next time put your false teeth in properly before coming to my table.' Bessie switches on the English Service of the SABC and happens to catch part of a political commentator's talk about the Prime Minister, Dr. Hendrik Verwoerd.

'Verwoerd is in favour of an ethnic democratic republic...'

'I don't want to hear about that old devil,' interjects Winnie.

But Bessie wants Winnie to calm down and behave, so she ups the volume and continues listening to a talk in which she has a scant interest, as the commentator continues.

'Since the days of the Dutch Batavian Republic at the Cape, the Afrikaners have cherished the idea of self-determination. The ideology of an ethnic democratic republic was fostered during the French Revolution and its form was influenced by the concept of the Western City State, such as those that existed in ancient Greece.'

'Oh, come now, Bessie, that's enough!'

Bessie turns up the volume another notch. 'But Dr. Verwoerd looked to more contemporary examples of separate development and found inspiration in the segregationist policies of the southern states of America...'

Winnie gets up. 'I'm off! I'm not listening to that rubbish!'

Bessie switches off the radio, looks sternly at her sister, saying emphatically, 'Now, as I was saying, if it weren't for their long-suffering maid, Agnes, that thing would be wallowing up to her eyebrows in filth.'

'That's really disgraceful!' Winnie asserts, resuming her role as a companionable Pollyanna.

'She's just a jumped-up thing from Point Road. Got no culture... nothing upstairs!'

Bessie takes a deep sigh, as if she has endured an exceptionally long penance, and would now like some light relief. 'Would you like a glass of sherry, Winnie?'

Like Pavlov's salivating dog, the sweet sound of the word sherry excites waves of desire within Winnie's brain cells, causing her to lick her lips with delight. 'I'd love some!'

Holding the bottle neck tightly, Bessie pours two generous glasses of sherry, as if draining the last drop of Susan's blood. 'She doesn't deserve to be a mother.'

'Are they planning to have more children?'

'The bitch is on her back every night... but only for pleasure. She doesn't want any more screaming brats, so George tells me.'

'Is she strict with Candice?'

'The other day she gave the poor child such a thrashing that she dirtied her frock.'

'Didn't you try to stop her?'

'Are you mad?' She'd sooner turn the strap on me. She's done that before today.'

'Really!'

'Not with a strap, but the hellcat flew at me one day with her claws outstretched because I had dared to suggest that Candice wasn't being properly fed.'

Bessie pauses her tirade as she hears the sound of a car pulling away from outside.

'Humph! There they go!' She peeks through the curtain. 'Humph! No, it's not them in the car. But look at that, I ask you, they're walking hand-in-hand down the pavement. Humph! Now that she's got him all to herself, she can feed him a pack of lies about me.'

'Shame Bess, it's not fair on you.'

'Perhaps it's just as well they're not going by car because the poor man can't enjoy the ride without her sitting on top of him. Hasn't a scrap of decency.'

'Yes, yes, of course. That's how accidents happen. These young women excite their menfolk on the road until they can't see straight. And then... bang!'

Bessie opens the fridge and takes out a wobbly jelly. 'I made this especially for George.'

She puts the green jelly on the table before turning to the wall mirror where she starts releasing her hair rollers. But after getting a few strands caught-up in the process, Winnie helps to untangle the mess. 'I did all this for George. I wanted to look nice for him.'

Winnie looks around for a comb.

'Don't worry, I'll just pat it down with my hands.'

'You've got lovely hair for your age. I wish my old thatch would look as good.'

Winnie is finding giddy pleasure in the sweet-tasting sherry and, in the hope of having more, is prepared to listen patiently to her sister's tirade. She sits down, glances at Bessie before opening the bottle of sherry, and gives a fake sympathetic expression on hearing more of her sister's litany of woes.

'I can't sleep some nights worrying myself sick about George, and the mess he's made of his life.'

'At least he's married, not like my Reg who's 37 next birthday and has done absolutely nothing with his life. He's still a crane operator on a building site in town. The man has brains but has never used them. Jennifer left him after five years. She wasn't going to stay married to a drunkard. He nearly lost his job the other day after dropping a load of bricks on the road.'

Bessie listens with half an ear as the photograph of her and George on the mantelpiece is far more engrossing.

'It's a wonder my poor George hasn't been driven to drink.'

Winnie excuses a hiccup before taking another gulp of sherry.

Bessie starts clearing the table while Winnie quickly snitches a piece of lamb from the serving plate before it's taken away.

'Why doesn't George do something about the situation?'

'Every time the poor man opens his mouth, he gets his head bitten off. Have some more sherry.'

Winnie's eyes droop, but she can't resist the offer. 'Just a drop, otherwise I'll be passing out on your couch tonight.'

'You can't have a decent conversation with the witch. She just sits and puffs herself up like an engorged pufferfish.'

Winnie starts giggling again.

Bessie ignores her and ends up talking to herself in the mirror while patting down strands of loose hair. 'Don't get me wrong, I'm not running the bitch down because she's stupid, I'm not one for running anyone down, as you know. But she just makes me so angry.'

'Shame! Poor old, George.'

Bessie returns to the table and unpins a brooch from her dress. 'George gave me this for my birthday. Nice, isn't it? He's got good taste, has my George.'

'It's lovely, Bessie.'

'But this thing next door nearly had a cadenza when she saw it because he hadn't given her one, too. Such pettiness, I ask you! Of course, he doesn't know what's being sent to the old cow in Pretoria.'

'What old cow's that, Bessie?'

A knock at the front door interrupts their conversation.

'I know what's being sent that end, but I daren't say a word.'

Bessie ignores the knocking.

'There's someone at the door...' hiccups Winnie.

'Her blerry mother, that's who!'

'Oh, is she coming tonight?'

'Half the housekeeping money is sent to that old crone, and that's why poor Candice has to starve.'

The knocking gets louder and more urgent.

Wanting to deflect attention away from the knocking, Bessie says, 'It's disgraceful, don't you think, Winnie?'

'Aren't you going to open the door?'

'Not tonight, Winnie, not tonight.'

'Why not tonight?' asks Winnie with her eyes bulging and stifling a bubbly belch.

'Just that! I'm not opening the door tonight.'

The knocking continues and a voice is heard, 'Bessie, it's me!'

'But... it's... it's...' says Winnie, recognizing the voice.

'Keep your voice down! I'm not letting that idiot in at this time of night. I'm not in the mood.'

Chapter 2

A Night Out

At night the Durban beachfront is a world apart from the rest of the city; cloaked in a romantic mystique of eclectic colours and shades that excites the senses, making a dinner-for-two all the more intimate. The Charcoal Haven, the venue chosen by George for an intimate tryst, is tucked away in a narrow thoroughfare connecting Gillespie Street with the Snell Parade. This low, flat roofed, cosy restaurant is where he and Susan are to celebrate their 5th wedding anniversary. It has a unique charm and ambience that diners enjoy. George and Susan make a handsome couple, with Susan looking particularly striking in her sexy black mini skirt, red chiffon blouse and flip-bob Jackie Kennedy hairstyle, with George in black slacks and blue open neck shirt.

Susan is given a warm greeting from the Indian Head Waiter who ushers them to a table overlooking the narrow, shadowy lane. He greets her as Miss Susan, which elicits a double take from George, who, after ordering a bottle of sparkling wine, suggests inquisitively, 'You seem to be well known here.'

Susan hesitates for a moment before giving him a disarming smile. 'Hazel and I had a birthday lunch here last week.'

George wants to make this a special evening and produces from his jacket pocket a small velvet-coated black box. Susan smiles, suspecting jewellery. 'What's that?'

He slips on a silver bracelet with three large charms depicting a lion, lioness and a cub, the reverse sides engraved with their respective names.

'And our little Candice, the cub charm,' she smiles. 'Thank you, it's lovely, ' and stretches across the table to kiss him.

Knowing how much Susan enjoys seafood they both order crayfish thermidors, and don't bother to check the price.

Susan becomes uncomfortably aware of a man sitting on the far side of the restaurant staring at her. She is used to getting admiring glances, but this man won't take his eyes off her. She asks George to change places, making an excuse about the overhead light in her eyes. After a sip of sparkling wine and a deep inhalation of her king-size Peter Stuyvesant filter-tipped cigarette to calm her nerves, she begins to settle down.

'Is there anything upsetting you?'

'No, no, it's been a tiring day, and I was so looking forward to this evening with you.'

She stubs out the half-smoked cigarette, leans across the table and says appealingly, 'George... don't you think it's time for us to move on?'

'What do you mean?'

'We've been living in the same house for our entire marriage. I know you love calling it a house, but it's a maisonette – two homes locked under one roof with two separate entrances.' She shakes her head in disapproval. 'I think it's time we moved on.'

'But it's enabled us to save.'

She is not placated by this reply, but George believes it serves their interests to stay on. 'I reckon we should stay on for at least another year,' he persuasively suggests.

Susan reacts glumly as she dreads having to spend another year so close to an interfering, nagging mother-in-law. 'Your mother thinks the sun shines out of your backside. You can do no wrong in her eyes, but it's very frustrating and irritating for me.'

'I told you not to take her comments seriously. Since my father died, I've been all she's had and now that I'm no longer living with her, she's lonely.'

'She's got her sister and that crazy fellow on the bicycle who fancies her.' Susan takes another sip of wine. 'I hate going there as I'm always made to feel unwelcome. She treats me like an inferior... that I'm not good enough for her precious son.'

'Just stick it out a little longer... please, for my sake.'

'She's driving a wedge between us... and it's not good for Candice.'

'Come now, she's a doting grandmother. They're all the same.'

'My mother doesn't interfere.'

'Your mom lives in Pretoria.'

'I'm telling you, George, for your sake I'll stick it out for one more year and not a minute longer, and then we must be out of there... okay? Do you promise?'

George reluctantly nods agreement.

'Otherwise, Candice and I are out of there.'

'That's rather radical!'

'You give me no option... I'm not prepared to lose another night's sleep mulling over the unsatisfactory arrangement of her constant spying and uncalled for criticism of everything I say and do.'

'Don't tell me that's why you've started taking sleeping tablets?'

Susan doesn't answer.

George feels threatened by her comment and looks around the restaurant hoping to see something that could take the conversation in a different direction. As a motorcar salesman he knows that he can get a job anywhere in the country should he wish to move. But he is quite happy at the moment and earns a decent salary with commission. After an awkward silence, he says, 'What I like about this place is the atmosphere. So, let's enjoy it.'

Susan doesn't reply and continues to sense the intense gaze of the man at the opposite end of the restaurant. George lights up a cigarette, 'I'm not wanting to move too far from the beachfront. Perhaps we could look at a flat on the far side of North Beach.'

He still cannot elicit a flow of conversation, so he touches on a subject that has concerned him of late. 'I've noticed that you spend a lot of time away from our home during the day. Is it your marketing job, or because of my mother?'

'What do you mean, a lot of time?' Susan replies defensively, jolting her mind back to the present with a slight tone of anxiety.

George looks directly at her, 'I'm sorry to quote my mother, but she says you leave the house before lunch and come back in the late afternoon. This could be as often as three times a week.'

'You see what I mean, George? Your mother's a prying old… I won't say what I think, but she must keep her bloody nose out of my life.'

'So, where *do* you go? You don't do market research all day?'

'I've got friends! We go out… to the beach… to the movies. Or do you want me to sit around all day in the house and rot?'

'Course not, but there's Candice that you could pick up earlier in the afternoon and save me the trip.'

'She's very happy at the all-day nursery school, interacting with other children and I have no intention of taking her out early as there are no children to play with where we live.'

George feels the emotional temperature rising as Susan's voice pitches high and sharp. 'What do you want from me, George? Full-time slavery?'

He pulls back in his chair and takes a deep draw on his cigarette. His mind is a whirl of confusion about Susan's relationship with his mother and her long hours spent away from home. When he started dating her, his mother would call her all sorts of horrible names hoping to destroy the relationship, saying that she was unworthy to be his wife. But he would have none of it, and the more she tried to dissuade him from marrying Susan, the more determined he was to do so. He recalls one eventful evening shortly after their engagement when Bessie made a final attempt to destroy the relationship. It ended in such a fierce row that neighbours felt almost obliged to call the police. Not having succeeded then, his mother changed her tactics by feeding him with ideas of divorce, even encouraging him to leave Susan once Candice was born. But leaving Susan is not something George is prepared to consider; he loves both her and Candice dearly, and wants his marriage to succeed. At the same time, his devotion and loyalty to his mother are unquestionable. There has always been a strong bond between them ever since he was a toddler. In the ensuing years, Bessie has come to depend on her son not only as a companion but someone who would always be around. She has become an integral part of his life and George sees no reason why that should change… it is an unquestioning acceptance of the status quo that has completely blindsided him to the strain that it is putting on his marriage.

George pays the bill and they stroll out of the restaurant initially holding hands, but Susan drops his hand as they pass a table near the door where the man who had been staring at her is sitting. She looks straight ahead.

By the time they reach their front door they are on the same giddy wavelength with George steering her to the bedroom where all negative thoughts of his mother have been swept aside in anticipation of an erotic climax to their anniversary.

Next morning, George is up early and goes fishing with his two mates, Graham and Basil, and doesn't return until late afternoon with a catch of four shad, one of which is prepared for supper that night, the other is given to Bessie and the remaining two are put in the freezer.

Susan is not one for staying at home when a sunny beach beckons and she spends that Sunday morning with Candice and her close friend Hazel Jones on the golden sands of South Beach, both disporting sexy bikinis. As Hazel is unmarried, she willingly attracts suitable male attention and soon saunters off with a handsome young man to the XL Tearoom for snacks.

With Susan sitting alone next to Candice building a sandcastle, another young fellow invites himself to sit next to her. She almost utters, 'Hello, Derek,' but then notices this fellow doesn't have a left arm tattoo.

'I nearly confused you with someone else. He looks very similar.'

'We all have our doubles,' he laughs, and orders hamburgers from a passing beach vendor. After building a large, wobbly sandcastle with the help of the young chap, Candice shows signs of boredom after the castle collapses and wants to go home. They stroll back to the house where Susan invites the young fellow inside for coffee. Buster, as he calls himself, is a good-looking chap, who works for a large electrical company, and, as a journeyman electrician, he is clued-up on plugs and wiring and offers to install a double plug in the kitchen when he has some free time.

Shortly afterwards, Hazel and her companion pop in briefly and the four young adults enjoy a pleasant time chatting and sharing a packet of hot potato chips. Susan ushers them out before 4 o'clock knowing that George is likely to return at about that time.

On Wednesday morning, Buster returns to install the kitchen plug. He is a very gregarious and presentational young man; his opening comment impresses Susan. 'When a lady calls, I am fully charged to be at her service.'

She is struck by the uncanny resemblance to his twin brother Derek and has to correct herself once or twice in getting the name right.

'It's okay if you call me Derek, as long as you know that it's me that you're dealing with.'

Susan blushes but doesn't wish to pursue that conversation further. He finds Susan very sexy and hopefully accommodating, and instinctively flexes his biceps in her presence knowing how some women are drawn to muscular men.

'Would you like a cup of coffee, big boy?'

'Never say no to a little stimulation.'

He tells her that he is a member of the Rovers Rugby Club, often playing left flank or eighth man. 'I love to pack down in a tight scrum… what I call, caught in a bum jam,' and crudely laughs.

Buster goes to the kitchen with the confidence of someone who knows his way around the house, puts his toolbox down next to the plug point and smilingly intones a double-entendre. 'You won't regret having a double plug. Yeah, a lot of women I know enjoy getting it both ends,' punctuating his remark with a smirk and a wink.

Erotic feelings begin to stir within Susan and everything he says thereafter ignites hidden sexual desires. Although she knows that she should hold her wild desires in check, she finds Buster very appealing and his rugged good looks are a strong magnetic attraction.

Susan has a way of compartmentalizing her mind between motherhood and wife and being able to firmly push both aside depending on the moment. But she does sense possible danger in having Agnes the maid in the house, so she quickly runs up a grocery list and sends her to the supermarket. This tactic is not lost on Buster, who senses an opportunity to take advantage of what he thinks is a frustrated housewife looking for a bright spark to light up her dull life.

He switches off the mains to remove the single plug and sets about replacing it with a double. He breathes gently and audibly over his screwdriver, the sexual innuendo is not lost on Susan, who places two cups of hot coffee on the kitchen table. She visually interrogates this rugged looking young man whose age she guesses to be about 25. As a sportsman and regular beachgoer, he has an attractive glowing, healthy tanned complexion.

'Do you enjoy watching rugby?' he asks.

'Not really.'

'You must come and watch Natal play Transvaal next Saturday. I can organize tickets.'

'Can't promise. Weekends are difficult to manage unless my man goes fishing.'

'Think about it… we've got a good team. Izak van Heerden is a great coach. He managed the Springboks against the Lions earlier this year. Great guy!'

Rugby is not a conversation piece that holds Susan's attention, who is riveted on Buster's masculinity, admiring his rippling biceps as he applies exaggerated pressure to a stubborn screw. 'Is this what you want to do with your life?' she asks blandly, not having any other suitable question in mind.

'Yeah, I love it! The pay's okay, and I'm planning to team up with my brother as he seems to be doing very well for himself.'

Susan blushes at the mention of Derek, as she has known him for about a year, and is fully aware of his line of business.

Buster sits down next to Susan, sugars his coffee and takes a leisurely sip of the strong aromatic brew.

'You're a very beautiful woman,' he croons, while slowly stirring his coffee with a hand that is longing to touch her. 'Has anyone ever told you that?' he asks in his deep baritone voice, relying on his trusty opening liner to ignite a spark of interest.

'Not recently, no.'

'Well, I think you are the most desirable woman I have met in a long time, and I have met many women, but none with your beauty.'

Somehow, five years of marriage and a child disappears from her consciousness, as she gazes into Buster's dark brown eyes. He stands, wanting to usher her to the bedroom, but when they get to the bedside, Susan panics believing that her marriage bed is not the place to do it.

'Sorry, Buster... but... I've just remembered I have to pick up my daughter in twenty minutes,' which is a lie as George will do that after work at 4.30.

Buster doesn't push the advances any further, believing that this is a risky place to have sex with a married woman.

'Look, I've got a flat just off the Marine Parade. What say you, I'll come around on Friday morning, and pick you up?'

'That's a much safer bet with Candice at school.'

Buster returns to the kitchen and before gathering his tools, gives Susan a passionate embrace and a lingering French kiss.

He whispers in her ear, 'Ten o'clock, Friday.'

She gives him an alluring smile, knowing that she has this fellow under her spell.

'Until then,' he says, huskily.

'Until then,' she murmurs sexily, tossing back her tousled hair.

Chapter 3

Mr. Blignaut

It is mid-morning and Winnie is again visiting her sister to help re-arrange pieces of furniture in the lounge. They move a large, imbuia dining room table to a position next to the front window overlooking Prince Street.

'Why do you want people looking at you while you eat?'

'I can always close the curtains,' Bessie replies. 'But I need to see what's happening on my doorstep.'

'You mean, George's doorsteps,' replies Winnie with a sardonic smile.

Not wanting to be considered a spying mother-in-law, Bessie shrugs her shoulders saying, 'I'm so grateful for your help Winnie. I couldn't have done this on my own.'

A knock at the front door interrupts their chat.

'Now, who could that be, I wonder?' asks Bessie as she moves across the lounge to open the door. Framed in the doorway is a slender grey-haired man in his late fifties, looking somewhat ridiculous holding a bunch of wilting flowers in one hand and two sealed paper packets in the other.

'Hello, Bess,' he grins.

'Oh, it's you!'

'Yes, I called the other night, but you may have been out.' He gives the flower petals a gentle tickle, saying to them, 'You need to wake up and look fresh for the lady.'

'You know me by now, I never open the door after dark.'

With a winsome smile, he comes right up to her, 'You mean not even for me?'

'Come inside, there's a draught.'

'I thought we could have a nice glass of... '

She shakes her head, scowling at him.

'Then let's make it a cup of coffee and a chat.'

'I get enough chat from my sister without any additional yapping from you, thank you very much.'

Winnie looks longingly at the bottle as she doesn't confine her drinking to set hours.

Mr. Blignaut steps inside giving his bottom a little shake, a peculiar mannerism he acquired as a youngster on a Transvaal poultry farm where he was told by his mother to shake the dust off his pants before stepping inside. So, he copied one of the hens that perfected the technique of feather dusting her bottom with a good shake. But his entrance ritual is not complete until he stoops to pull off the metal spring clips around his trouser legs that keep the ends of his flannels from getting caught in the bicycle chain. He then stands to attention to give the two ladies a big toothy grin. He was once married to an Afrikaans girl, who left him many years ago after falling in love with a young electrician. She and Charlie had no children and she considered his clerical job at the Post Office to be a boring dead-end occupation unbefitting her imagined status.

Charlie shakes a reprimanding finger at his bicycle, 'Listen here, old Chooks, you let me down on the way here.' Frowning, he turns to the two women, 'I had to walk half the way from the Post Office. Her chain kept slipping off.'

'Serves you right, peddling around on that piece of old rubbish,' Bessie snaps in a crusty tone of voice.

'Now that's no way to talk about my old Chooks.'

'Oh, stop complaining you old booze lizard and sit down.'

Charlie holds out the bunch of flowers, but Bessie makes no effort to take them, so he puts them on the sideboard.

Winnie, who has been observing the scene, chirps, 'Bessie,

be careful, he's hiding things behind his back.'

'What are you hiding this time, Charlie Blignaut? More alcohol?'

'I can see it,' blurts Winnie, in a telltale voice. 'It's a bottle of wine... and there's something else he's holding... also in a brown packet.'

'Wine!' Bessie exclaims with disgust! 'At this time of the day!'

'It's supposed to be a surprise,' he announces with a supercilious grin.

'Surprise! We don't need any surprises here, thank you very much. We're not a couple of old trollies that need to be jazzed-up with a cheap bottle of hooch.'

'Come now, Bess,' he whines, 'I thought you could invite me to lunch so we could settle into a nice lovey-dovey afternoon.'

Winnie looks on most disapprovingly.

'But if that doesn't take your fancy... then let's just have a dop and be happy.'

Getting no response from Bessie, he turns to Winnie. 'What do you say Win?' Winnie's eyes light up, as she has a soft spot for Charlie, who has the most appealing blue eyes that she can't resist.

'Don't pay any attention to him, Winnie. He's come straight from the bar I can smell it.'

'Oh, naughty boy,' says Winnie with a cheeky smile.

'And I can also smell something else. Phew!' Bessie screws up her nose, adding, 'What's in that brown paper packet? A dead fish?'

'Ah, that!'

Charlie is mortified and quickly takes the packet that he had left on the dinner table and puts it outside the front door on the top step.

'I'll collect it on my way out,' he says with embarrassment, closing the door and fanning his nose.

'Is it your lunch?' asks Winnie.

'No, I wouldn't eat that.'

'What is it then?'

Clearing his throat and looking at the ground, 'It's a... a specimen.'

'A what!' exclaims Bessie.

'I've been getting a lot of tummy cramps lately, so the quack wants to check my stool.'

Bessie splutters in disgust, 'You mean to say that you brought a piece of your waste matter into my house... and put it on my dining room table? How dare you! Filthy beast!' She is nearly choking with rage.

Winnie starts giggling, which Charlie takes as a sign of sympathy that encourages him to put an arm around her.

'Goodness sake, Winnie! Don't let the brute touch you!'

Winnie, who has emptied many a bedpan in her time as a nurse, doesn't protest. He looks into her hazel eyes. 'You know, Bessie, you have a very attractive sister.'

Following an unsuspecting peck on the cheek from Charlie, Winnie giggles. 'I think he's just trying to be sociable, Bessie.'

Charlie delivers a disarming smile, and his blue eyes light up his craggy face, 'That's my girl, Win.'

'Don't encourage the swine, Winnie.'

Charlie whispers into Winnie's ear, 'I think she's jealous.'

He leaves Winnie and moves to sit down next to Bessie. 'Not so, Bess, you're jealous.'

'Sis!'

'It's always sis with you, hey, Bessie! So, what's it this time?'

'Your breath! Peppermint beer!'

Charlie opens the bottle of wine in front of Bessie, declaring that she doesn't know what she's missing. With the bottle held aloft, he does a little Irish jig and tries to entice her to have some. 'There you go, it's down the hatch one, two, three – touch your toes and off you go on a flying trapeze.'

Bessie ignores him and turns on the radio for the one o'clock news, picking up a portion of the opening headline.

'... he will be moved from Marshall Square in Johannesburg to Pretoria to stand trial.'

'Who's he talking about?' asks Winnie.

The announcer continues, 'Mandela is charged with inciting workers to strike and leaving the country without permission.'

'That troublemaker should be locked up,' Bessie snorts cuttingly, slapping a loaf of fresh white bread on the table.

'Turn it off, Bessie, we don't want to hear about that.'

Bessie obliges, and they all sit down to lunch, with Bessie still harping on about her pet subject, 'If she'd only leave the poor man alone for one minute.'

Charlie absent-mindedly asks, 'Who? Mandela?'

Bessie ignores him. He gets up to open the wine bottle, sees no glasses so uses the teacups. Adopting the attitude of a polite wine steward, he says to Winnie in a posh voice, 'A drop for the sweet, pretty lady?' She giggles and coyly coos back with a chirping tone, 'Thank you, Mr. Blignaut.'

Then, changing the tone of his voice to that of an army major-general, he declares boldly, 'And now one gigantic dop for old Bess.'

'Mr. Blignaut, for your information, I'm not an old carthorse that has to be doped up on booze. And, by the way, those were put out for the tea.'

'That's okay, I've left you the saucers.'

Bessie rises to fetch wine glasses and while she's out of the room Winnie says, 'Come and sit over here Mr. Blignaut....'

'Call me, Charlie.'

'Only when I know you better,' she replies in a simpering voice.

He places his chair next to hers and leaning perilously over, puts his arm around her. When Bessie returns with the glasses, Winnie pulls away with Charlie toppling off the chair and onto the floor. Regaining his dignity, he quickly changes the subject saying with an impish voice, 'Nice glasses, yes, very nice.'

'Talk sense, you idiot.'

With a swift change of tone, he says, 'You know, Bessie, I've been reading about our local hero, Captain Edwin Swales, who completed one of the most successful bombing raids over Germany during the war.'

'What on earth are you jabbering about now?'

'The war!'

'Which one?' asks Bessie in a cheeky tone.

'The second... the one that I took part in.'

'Then give us the facts, and stop beating about the bush,' she snaps curtly.

'Captain Swales was piloting an aircraft that was so badly shot out by the Germans, that he barely made it to the French border.'

Showing a total lack of interest, Bessie turns to Winnie, 'What's the weather like outside today, Win? I haven't had a chance to go out.'

But Charlie is not to be put off his stride. 'The bad weather put further stress on Swales' damaged plane.'

'It's a good day to do the washing,' replies Winnie, trying to bring the conversation down to Bessie's level of interest.

Bessie turns sharply on Charlie. 'I don't want to hear about bad weather.'

'I'm just telling you about a chap who showed heroic courage... in bad weather. What he did, Bessie, was nothing short of heroic virtue.'

'Virtue? My, my, that's a fine word coming from your filthy mouth.'

'Why do you want to mock this chap? What he did was heroic. Do you know that he managed to get his crew to bail out to safety before the bomber crashed... yes it crashed, killing him instantly.'

Winnie gives him a winsome smile. 'That's a lovely story, Charlie... I mean, Mr. Blignaut.'

He smiles appreciatively. 'He gave his life so that his colleagues may live. Who does that every day?'

The three of them settle down to a couple more glasses of semi-sweet Lieberstein wine, which releases both the best and the worst in them. Charlie is flattered by Winnie's charms, but it's Bessie with whom he really wants to make a good impression. 'You must come out with me someday, Bess.'

'The day you can afford a motor car is the day I will go out with you,' she asserts, feeling the early effects of the wine.

'I was hoping you'd settle for a tandem.'

She knits her brow in disgust.

'I know a bloke who said he could convert my old Chooks into a snazzy two-seater tandem.'

'I wouldn't be seen dead on that thing,' Bessie snaps.

'Oh, I wouldn't mind,' chirps Winnie.

Still trying his best to impress Bessie, he declares, 'If it's a car you want Bess, then a car you'll have.'

She laughs scornfully at his promise. 'You don't have enough money to buy a spare wheel.'

'Just you wait and see, Mrs. Cooksley. I'll make you eat your words.'

Charlie looks at his watch and exclaims, 'I must be off. I have to get my specimen to the quack before 4 o'clock.'

He bends forward to kiss Bessie, but she deliberately leans back, and he nearly topples over. Winnie rushes forward to help him straighten up, and when their eyes meet, he gives her a smacking kiss on the mouth while giving Bessie a sideways glance.

'That won't work with me Mr. Charlie Blignaut,' Bessie declares with a scornful laugh.

'Farewell, ladies until we meet again.'

Winnie escorts him to the front door.

'Thank you, kind lady,' he says with the exaggerated charm of an aging Lothario.

She blushes, replying sweetly, 'Bye Charlie.'

He gives her a sexy wink and steps outside to see a dog licking its lips and the brown paper packet torn and empty.

'Oh, that wicked dog!' shrieks Winnie. 'He's a dreadful scavenger! Lives on the street and eats anything and everything he comes across.'

The dog nonchalantly walks a few metres down the pavement, pauses, and drops a turd. Bessie looks disgustedly at Charlie.

'Take that one… coming from you, the doctor wouldn't know the difference.'

'Sure thing, Bessie,' he guffaws, mounting his beloved Chooks, and furiously pedalling away. He waves back at her, shouting, 'I hope to get home in time to produce another specimen before 4 o'clock.'

She puckers her nose and slams the front door closed.

Chapter 4

A Bad Connection

A colourful kaleidoscope of myriad patterns and eye-catching objects captured in a plethora of entertaining and thrilling activities never fails to excite a child's imagination exposed to the Durban holiday beachfront. Fairground thrills, miniature train and pleasure boat rides, dodgem cars, and trips to mini-town have imprinted a profusion of life-long memorable delights in young Candice's mind. She particularly enjoys the annual visit of the circus with the irrepressible *Tickey the Clown* goofing about under the Big Top, adding to the squeals of delight that permeate the atmosphere of this part of town where pleasure-seeking children of all ages release their pent-up inhibitions. Even nearby roosting mynah birds add to this seasonal cacophony with their discordant screeching as if they too find subliminal pleasure in the crazy world below them. Protected and guided by George, Candice loves riding the hefty, foamy waves on inflatable rubber surf mats and hopes as a teenager to graduate to the more challenging traditional surfboard. The paddling pool and pedal-boat rides all feed into her magical playground, releasing swirls of adrenalin to imprint experiences that she will remember forever as a period of childhood innocence.

On the other hand, for young adults like Buster and Susan looking for gratification, there are the ladies' bars and floorshows to spike their erogenous zones and concupiscence. As a married woman, Susan is severely constrained in how she spends her evenings, but to be picked up during the daytime by Buster can easily be disguised and integrated into her daily marketing routine. But when Buster calls at about 9 o'clock, he is unaware that a middle-aged woman with the eyes of a hawk is keenly observing who goes in and out of her son's house next door. She takes note of the time that this strange, handsome man and Susan are seen leaving the house and getting into a car. Buster the extrovert makes flourishing gestures and beams big smiles as he drives her to his North Beach flat, leaving Bessie with alarm bells ringing in her warped imagination and conjuring suspicious intentions behind this outing.

Buster parks his car in an underground reserved parking bay before leading the way to his second-floor flat. Susan's heart is thumping, knowing that this is a potentially dangerous liaison with a man she doesn't know, notwithstanding that he is the twin brother of Derek whom she has known for about a year.

However, Susan is no stranger to casual hookups as she finds the excitement relieves the boring routine of married life, and sex with George is no longer exhilarating so the opportunity of finding new sex partners always generates a frisky thrill, plus the money is readily welcomed. She knows some couples talk about a seven-year itch, but she started scratching a lot sooner, five years to be exact.

Buster's bedroom wall is plastered with pictures of nearly nude, muscular men that she finds confusing, but assumes it is part of his fetish to be inspired by other male bodybuilders. Admiring his sun-tanned muscular and youthful physique, she visualizes lying naked next to this Adonis. A snap thought reminds her that she had taken a contraceptive pill that morning.

Out of sight, Buster offers her a drink adding to the liqueur brandy a sprinkling of the recreational drug LSD, that he got from his twin brother. Susan drinks it down quickly in the hope of suppressing her lingering sense of guilt but doesn't need any drug to spike her rising libido. She is fully aware of this being a purely physical encounter with no commitment and hopes there'll be no untoward consequences.

She likes to take control in these situations and starts to undress Buster while teasingly touching his muscular, tanned biceps and pecs in the process. She continues undressing this hunk as if he were a gift-wrapped offering of intense erotic delight. Buster slips off his underpants and stands in front of her with a grand style erection that he thrusts up against her stomach. Susan quickly undresses, and by the time she is naked, they are lying side-by-side on the bed. She closes her eyes, indulging in vivid sexual fantasies to enhance the purely physical act of intercourse.

But Buster's warped view of sex goes far beyond anything she has ever imagined let alone experienced… the rougher and dirtier the better. He forces Susan onto her knees thrusting his enlarged penis into her anal canal, hoping to give her the pleasure that he derives from such a disordered act. She resists and pushes him away. He reacts by grabbing her, forcing her to lie flat on her back and holding her hands above her head as he tries to thrust his penis into her mouth. She squirms away from him, leaps off the bed and runs to the bathroom to rinse her mouth, as he had managed to get past her lips.

'Hey, what are you doing, Su Boo?' he shouts angrily.

'You repulse me… disgusting beast!'

'Don't be such a bitch!' Laughing crudely, he taunts, 'the women I know like backdoor sex.'

'Who are they, prostitutes?' She spits out the last mouthful of rinsed water.

'Yes, like you!'

'I'm not a prostitute, I'm an escort.'

Buster raises his voice so she can hear him from the bathroom, 'Oh excuse me… a high-class prostitute. You know I could have sworn you were a high-class slut!'

Susan screams back, 'Shut up, you piece of shit!'

'See what I mean, shitty language from a shitty slut!'

She re-enters the bedroom while he sits on the bed leering

lustily at her body and begins masturbating. She quickly dresses and rushes to the front door, but he blocks her path, and with threatening blue eyes growls, 'Watch it, fucking bitch! I'll kill you! Nobody fucks me around... do you hear?'

Survival instinct kicks in as Susan draws on all her energy to push past him, slamming the door behind her as she heads for the street. But the effects of the hallucinatory drug are playing havoc with her senses, and she sees threatening and weird colours coming from moving objects like the radiators of passing cars vomiting rainbows over her; their colours shouting to her in a cacophony of strident voices. She hears bright colours of advertising billboards speaking to her in gibberish and hears the blue and white Surf washing powder advert swishing and swirling in a foamy seashore, washing her snowy white. She arrives at her front gate in tears, detected by her mother-in-law sitting at her spy window. She flings open the gate and hurries indoors. Bessie is alarmed to see her looking so wretched and bedraggled, and is inclined to go over and offer assistance, but decides against it believing that Susan would come to her if she needed help. Furthermore, she doesn't want to give the impression of spying on her daughter-in-law. However, these initial restraints are soon overwhelmed by a compulsive desire to find out what happened.

As Bessie has a key to Susan's front door, she brazenly walks in brushing past Agnes who looks shocked but says nothing, merely pointing to the bedroom door and shaking her head. Bessie knocks on the door but receives no response. She knocks again.

'Go away, Agnes! I don't want to be disturbed.'
'It's me, Susan, your mother-in-law.'
'Go away!'
'Can I make you some tea... or bring you something to eat?'

Susan is in a state of heightened agitation and imagines the room to be moving with the ceiling falling and rising above her. She pushes away these illusory phantoms, shouting, 'Go away!' With arms outstretched she shoves the ceiling off her chest.

Believing Susan to be drunk, Bessie tells Agnes to keep an eye on her and call her if it becomes urgent. She takes the maid by the arm, 'Come with me.'

Agnes follows her to the front porch.

'Who was this man I saw here this morning?'

'I'm not sure, madam. I think it's the same man who came the other day to fix the plug in the kitchen.'

'So, you don't know where he took her?'

'No, I was doing the washing in the back. I just heard his voice, but I think it's the same man.'

'Do other men come here during the day?'

'No, I don't see other men.

'You had best get on with your housework. I'm going next door to get some aspirin.'

Later when she returns with medication and a glass of water, Susan is sobbing and muttering incoherently.

'Here, Susan… here, take two of these. You'll get some sleep and feel much better.'

Susan's face is buried in her pillow and makes no effort to reply.

'Come, sit up.'

She props Susan up against her pillows and gives her the tablets. Susan looks dreadful and moans, 'I've got a splitting headache.'

'These will help.'

Bessie puts the remaining tablets on the bedside table and leaves, silently cursing that her poor George had married such a troubled and adulterous woman. On the way back to her maisonette, she bumps into Charlie Blignaut, who is walking swiftly along the pavement.

'What's the hurry?' she asks without really wanting to know.

'Everybody's standing in my way today,' he moans.

Side-stepping him, she replies, 'Well, don't let me stop you.'

'The darn police confiscated my Chooks because I was riding her on the pavement with no licence. So, they've put her in jail.'

Bessie looks at him as if he's touched in the head.

'She's locked up until I can pay the fine. And then some Bible puncher grabs hold of me and starts telling me that Jesus Christ started a church.'

'Which one?' Bessie asks distractedly and wanting to move on.

'That's what I said to this fanatic, who was standing dressed all in black in the hot sun oozing with holy oil.'

'Yeah, which one, I say,' Bessie repeats, without giving it much thought, and wanting to end the conversation.

'He tells me that Jesus started only one church and appointed his top apostle as its General Manager.'

'That's a new one on me.'

'He said he gave his GM authority to take important decisions which would be binding on earth and in heaven.'

'That's a tall order!'

'Yeah, and he assured me that today's GM sits in Rome and works off the same instruction sheet that was handed to old Peterkins the chief apostle.'

Bessie is not interested in what he is saying and tries to skirt around him.

'You're looking very agitated Bessie. What's up?'

'Nothing… nothing, I just don't have time to listen to your prattle.'

'I know you of old. You're hiding something.'

Bessie takes a deep breath to regain her composure, and exclaims with exasperation, 'Well, that must've been a complete waste of your time listening to such tripe, I'm sure.'

'Yeah, it was!'

He accompanies her the short distance to the front gate. 'Invite me inside, Bess, so we can have a quick *dop*. What do you say?'

She feels that she is very much in need of a strong drink, so, reluctantly nods and leads him inside.

'I've had a terrible day… and my poor old Chooks…'

'Come on now, just be quick. I have an appointment.'

Bessie throws open the lounge windows and turns on the light to brighten the dingy, low-ceiling room. She puts the remains of the Lieberstein on the table and brings out two glasses, which he fills to the brim and closes the curtains.

'What are you doing that for?'

'Come on there, Bess. I don't want to talk to you in bright sunlight. Have you got a candle?'

'A candle! Are you bloody mad?'

'Ja, a candle makes it all sexy like. You know, snoozie, boozie like.'

'Now, I know for sure Charlie Blignaut! You're stark raving mad!'

'Ag, come on there, Bess, give us a candle.'

'Don't be bloody stupid!'

He starts rummaging through the drawers of her sideboard.

'Stop messing about with my things! I'm not playing games with candles.'

'I promise to behave myself, Bess, promise. Just show me where they are.'

'Promise?'

'Promise.'

'Over there in the bottom drawer.'

Bessie keeps looking at her watch as if she has something urgent to do, while Mr. Blignaut is increasingly animated and pulls out a packet of Price's candles, removes two and sets them up on the table.

'Hey, you're making a mess with the wax.'

'They've got to stand up somehow.'

He looks around to see two tall glasses on top of the sideboard, which he uses as candle holders.

'Now, with the flick of a stick,' he lights the candles and moves to the electric light switch. 'And, with a flick of the switch,' he plunges the room into a dingy gloom, then gives Bessie a gentle slap on the bum.

'Stop that, you dirty brute!'

'Don't spoil it! I'm making it all cushy, mushy for you.' In a fake presentational voice, he declares, 'This is Bessie's Shangri-la and I'm her bird of paradise. Not so, Bess?'

She blows out the candles and shouts, 'Mr. Blignaut, turn the light on at once!'

'Charlie, Bess, call me, Charlie.'

'Come now, no funny business. I'm not in the mood for this,' she snaps with an irritated strained expression.

Charlie re-lights the candles but she blows them out again. Acting like a driven pyromaniac, he strikes another and another until Bessie yells at him. 'Stop this bloody nonsense, you'll set my house on fire.'

Standing in the middle of the room he announces, 'Music maestro! We must have music.'

Bessie sits back in despair while he rummages through a pile of Long-Playing Records before finding an old Vera Lynne favourite. He returns to the table with a dancing skip, a jump and a kick of the heels, 'Ah, listen to that songbird, Bess,' as Vera Lynne sings, *Keep the Home Fires Burning.*

'Mr. Blignaut, I think you'd better go home. You can't keep your promise to behave yourself.'

'But... but...'

'I don't trust you with the lights off.'

'But I want to say... yes, what I want to say is...'

'Go home! I know you want to say. You want to be dirty.'

With a beaming smile, he goes down on one knee in front of her, 'Bess, will you keep my home fires burning… you… grrrr…. beautiful beast of womanhood?'

She scowls.

'Will you come and live with me?'

'Never!'

'As my wife?'

'Forget it.'

The telephone rings, breaking the mood and bringing Bessie to her feet to answer it. He starts crawling on his knees behind her to the phone with hands held high in supplication, miming expressions of love. She covers the mouthpiece with her left hand to crack a sharp rebuke. 'Voetsek!' And gestures him to move away while she turns on a sweet welcoming voice.

'Hellooo...' and then pauses, 'Oh, it's you, Winnie!'

She holds the receiver away from her ear.

'No, I didn't tell you to *voetsek*. I'll phone you back later, I'm just putting out the rubbish.'

Bessie picks up her house keys, moves swiftly to the front door with Charlie trailing behind on his knees. She opens the door and gives him a kick in the butt saying, 'Go! Silly old arse! Find yourself a slut on Point Road.'

She quickly checks her watch and rushes back to Susan.

Chapter 5

Overdose

With a heavy anvil-topped cumulus nimbus cloud hanging overhead like a cloak of doom ready to engulf all that lies below, Durban awaits a late afternoon sub-tropical thunderstorm. A sharp zing of fresh ozone permeates the air as George gets out of the car and hurries across the road to pick up Candice from nursery school before the storm breaks.

'What's wrong, daddy? You look unhappy.'

'Mummy's not well.'

By the time they reach home, the rain buckets down and within seconds they are both drenched to the skin. But with her father at her side, Candice is not frightened by the deafening cracks of thunder and threatening streaks of lightning. Once inside the house, she looks momentarily out the window to watch the dramatic zig-zagging patterns of wild bolts of lightning flashing across the skyline.

Agnes summons George to the master bedroom where he sees his wife lying vacant-eyed in bed. He immediately phones his mother, while Agnes takes Candice to change into some dry clothes. When Bessie arrives with Winnie, she finds George in a state of distress. Susan is struggling to breathe, and her restless murmurings are interrupted by bouts of vomiting.

'What's happened?'

'I'm not sure. Agnes phoned me at work to tell me to come

home at once as Susan was very sick and mumbling a lot of nonsense.'

Winnie looks at the aspirin bottle on the bedside table, and then her eye catches an empty tablet bottle lying next to the bed. She quickly bends down to pick it up and gives a small gasp. 'Oh, my God!'

George's body stiffens as he hears what his aunt has to say. 'It's an empty bottle of sleeping tablets. It looks like she's tried to commit suicide.'

'Get an ambulance quick,' demands George.

Although Addington Hospital is diagonally across the road, Susan is far too ill to move her in the pouring rain. 'Help me prop her up,' pleads George.

Winnie puts another pillow under her head and tries to get Susan to sit up, but she is so weak that she simply flops to the side.

George shakes his head in despair. 'What on earth caused her to do this to herself?'

'She needs a stomach pump,' says Winnie, bringing her nursing experience to the fore.

When the ambulance arrives some fifteen minutes later the storm has abated, and Susan is driven with George to the casualty entrance, but Bessie and Winnie take brollies and walk the short distance. On the way, Bessie tells her sister about the strange man who visited Susan that morning, and how she had returned home highly distressed and possibly suicidal. 'If you ask me, she was in love with this man, who then dumped her.'

When they arrive at casualty, a doctor is busy treating Susan while George sits in a state of anxiety outside the emergency room.

'What's the verdict?'

'I haven't heard anything yet.'

Some ten minutes later, a doctor emerges from the room, 'Mr. Cooksley, you'd better step inside.'

Bessie wants to follow, but she is stopped. 'It's better if it's only the husband.'

The doctor closes the door behind leaving Bessie to return to her seat.

George is shocked to see Susan who is now unconscious, and her breathing is shallow and erratic.

'We have done all we can to empty the contents of her stomach and have treated her with medication.'

'Can't you operate?'

'She's too weak to survive an anaesthetic. There is nothing more we can do. Had she been admitted earlier we could have possibly saved her, but... but it's now too late.'

George looks down at his dying wife, feeling helpless. The doctor is moved by his grief. 'I'll be outside if you need me,' leaving George alone gently holding Susan's hand. 'Oh, Susie, my love! Why?'

Her eyes open slightly, and she looks almost pleadingly at him, but her pulse continues to rapidly weaken, and within minutes her life slips away leaving George holding a limp hand. His heart aches like never before. The excruciating emotional pain is almost unbearable. After tearfully kissing Susan goodbye, he leaves the room feeling a vast emptiness and sense of meaninglessness.

Bessie immediately reads the situation and embraces him, 'I'm so sorry, my son.'

Bessie scrambles for words. 'But perhaps in the long run … it's for the best.'

George freezes and gives his mother a steely, cold stare. Winnie embraces him, 'I'm so sorry, George …truly, so very sorry.'

They walk back to George's house in silence where they prepare to break the news to Candice.

That evening, Candice is given a light supper at Bessie's house while George, who is too grief-stricken, stays behind filled with aching emotions that can find no outlet and no answers. Numbed by shock, the next few days have a macabre dream-like quality in which he is a transient figure existing but not living. He searches deep within himself for reasons why Susan would have taken her life and begins to blame himself for not listening more carefully when she said she wanted to move to a home of their own, away from his mother. But surely that was not sufficient reason to kill herself... there had to be something else that had driven her to take such a drastic step and he was determined to find out what it was.

Bessie is deeply concerned at the way Susan's death has affected her beloved son and steps in to take care of all the funeral arrangements which include contacting Susan's family. She moves into the role of a surrogate mother to Candice who cannot comprehend her mother's absence.

'When is my mummy coming home, Granny?'

Bessie can't bear to look Candice in the face. 'I don't know my sweetie.'

'I hope she'll be home tonight because my daddy looks very sad.'

Bessie tucks the little girl into bed, without answering.

Candice's blue eyes moisten with tears. She wipes her cheeks with the back of her hands.

Susan's parents, as well as her brother and sister, arrive from Pretoria for the funeral and book in at the nearby Grand Hotel. They are all stunned by the turn of events because this is not the Susan they know; they were convinced she was happily married, and they all knew how much she loved her daughter. The questions come fast and furiously, but there are no satisfactory answers. George is a broken man who is as confused as they are. The funeral is a small family and close friends' affair. Winnie and Charlie are seated in the back row and Susan's friend, Hazel Jones, is sitting by herself near the front. Candice is seated next to George and Bessie. In George's mind, what is happening around him is surreal and he has occasionally to remind himself where he is and what purpose he had in being there. No pallbearers are needed as the coffin is already inside the tiny chapel. As death was never a subject of serious discussion in their home, George has no idea what Susan's preference would have been regarding burial or cremation. He had given the hired minister a note regarding the highlights of

Susan's short life, so he doesn't have any concern about what is to be said. But hearing the minister's words spoken sinks into his consciousness, setting off many reminiscent thoughts of their life together. His mind wanders back to the last night they had together and her plea to find a home away from his mother. He remembers how she would often say, 'Your mother doesn't think I'm good enough for you,' and he would brush it off, 'if you had to believe everything my mother has to say, you'd be in a lunatic asylum.' He is glad that he mostly took Susan's side in disagreements she had with his mother, though never forgetting how sometimes the arguments ended in extremely tense and emotional moments. He recalls the time shortly before the wedding how Bessie had tried to persuade him to break it off. 'Better one broken heart now, my son, than more to consider later.' But these thoughts are quickly pushed aside as coming from a mother who, as a single parent, had always put her son's interests first, just as she was doing at this particular moment in his life when he needed her support the most.

After the service, Hazel, Winnie and Charlie accompany George in his car to Stellawood Cemetery, with several other mourners going with members of Susan's family who had come down from Pretoria in two cars. The Minister talks about the chief animating principle of life, the immortal soul.

'A transcendental soul can never be destroyed,' he declares, 'but will live on forever depending on its state of grace in which it left this world.' Looking at George with consoling eyes, he says, 'Susan has merely undergone a transitional change to a new dimension of existence.'

Although George's mind and heart never embraced Christian beliefs, he is consoled by these words. He had acquired a smattering of religious doctrine that filtered through the educational system, but nothing stuck. However, at this moment, his mind begins to visualize a heavenly domain so vast that it would take forever to tour. He wishes that he and Susan could one day be together in such an ever-expanding universe and to set off on a grand unending celestial tour. He is quickly shaken out of his reverie by Charlie who takes him aside to offer his condolences. 'I rushed to the hospital when I heard the news, but I got lost and ended up in the maternity section, where a fussy old nurse mistook me for an agitated husband.'

George merely smiles knowing how confused Charlie can sometimes be. 'She opened the door to a woman lying in bed holding a newborn,' saying, 'congratulations father.'

George shakes his head.

'No, no, I said, that's not mine, and fled down the corridor. But the nurse caught up with me saying that I shouldn't be so rude.'

'Shame Charlie! You could have had a ready-made family.'

'Forget it! I wasn't her husband and if they couldn't find one, the woman must've had a virgin birth, and that's not my scene.'

After the service, Bessie invites everyone to her house for refreshment. George drives back home with the same occupants he took to the cemetery. He chats to Susan's family who, by and large, are very fond of him. Although they had received letters from Susan about his mother's dislike of her, they had not paid much attention to it until now. But such additional negative factors could have impacted Susan's mental state causing her to commit suicide Mrs. Thomas believes. Arriving at the repast, she is very cool in her greeting of Bessie and is quite rude to her at one point when she refuses to accept a slice of cake and moves away abruptly.

On talking to Hazel, George is introduced to another scenario when she mentions this fellow Buster, who took a fancy to Susan when they met on South Beach. All Hazel knows, however, is that on Susan's request he had gone to their house to fit a new kitchen plug. George is left wondering about all these unexplained factors, with none of them making any coherent sense. So, he decides to find out more about this elusive fellow, Buster, as any information would help come to an understanding of what drove his wife to commit suicide.

Chapter 6

On the Warpath

It's 7 November 1962, and in the background of Charlie's large communal office at the GPO the disembodied voice of the SABC newsreader announces, *Nelson Mandela has been sentenced to five years in prison for incitement and illegally leaving the country….* Charlie listens with half an ear but his main concern is for his old Chooks that the City Police had impounded because it was unlicensed, and the brake cable had snapped making it unroadworthy. He requests an extended lunch break to visit the City Police's vehicle pound where he fits a new brake cable and grudgingly pays the fine. After carefully checking for scratches and damage, he rides away speaking soothing words of comfort to his dear Chooks. He returns to the main Post Office, chains his 'sweetheart' to the bicycle rack inside the premises, and takes his lunch box across to the Town Gardens where he finds a comfortable shady spot on the lawn near the statue of Field Marshal Jan Smuts. As he begins to relax, his mind wanders back some twenty years when he was a young soldier who had enlisted in the army and served, up North, with the South African 2nd Infantry Division that was captured at Tobruk in 1942. He fondly recalls the camaraderie and bonding he had experienced among his fighting colleagues, and although he never joined the MOTH organization (Memorable Order of Tin Hats) on his return from the war, he has regularly attended the annual Remembrance Day service at the nearby Cenotaph. His mind rolls back to the victory parade that he was part of through the streets of Durban, and how he and other fighting men had been treated as heroes.

He looks up at the statue of Smuts, the great wartime leader and one of the founding members of the United Nations, and pays a silent tribute to the man who was once idolized by the majority of Afrikaners for his heroic deeds during the Anglo Boer War, but later spurned by many of them when he sided with Britain in the First World War.

Among Charlie's drinking pals, who all greatly admire Smuts, are several ex-World War II veterans who joined the MOTHs, and although he supports their charitable cause and purpose of true comradeship, mutual help, and sound memory, he has always preferred to be independent of any organized body. Charlie believes he has a sound memory, although he does confess to hyperbolize many of his wartime yarns.

His sound memory has not forgotten the local Bible puncher who pursued him halfway down the block the other day. So, when this fanatical street evangelist approaches him in the Town Gardens, he wants to throw a rock at him. Charlie looks closely at this bearded man in his late fifties, dressed in a long black cloak in the heat of a summer's day, and is reminded of the mad Russian monk, Rasputin. Of course, not everyone thinks Rasputin was mad, but as a bearded mystic, he certainly didn't act normally.

'Bless you, my good man, you didn't allow me to complete my message when we last met.'

'Go away, I'm having my lunch and reading my book.'

'What I have to say is more important than your lunch. Jesus, as God in flesh, spent 40 days fasting in the desert... think of that, and he never left behind a book.'

Charlie opens his book and picks up where he left off.

'No, sir, the Bible came 250 years after the good Lord left this earth, but what he did leave behind was a church.'

Lifting his face off the page, Charlie snaps, 'Go away, you're giving me indigestion.'

'Are you a good person, sir?'

'Piss off!

'We all like to think we're good unless you've gone too far down the slippery slope. But sir, how can anyone claim to be good, when most of us sin at least seven times a day.'

Charlie purposely stuffs his sandwich down his throat, expressing a threatening Maori haka war-face.

'Yes, sir, you may well grimace, but gluttony is one of the cardinal sins we sometimes commit. But there are more serious ones, such as pride and anger. Have you ever been guilty of intense anger when you wanted to murder someone?'

'Yes, I have that feeling right now.'

'Then you should be remorseful and ask God for forgiveness.'

'I have my own understanding of God. I don't need you to tell me.'

'In that case, sir, you have created an idol because no human mind can ever possibly comprehend the full extent of Almighty God. He's certainly not an old bearded fellow sitting on a cloud in the sky. He is way… way… beyond our understanding.'

'I don't need you or your church, or any church for that matter, to tell me how to live my life. I hate organized religion.'

'Then, welcome to the disorganized religions of the world, where today every denomination declares its understanding of the gospels to be true.'

Charlie starts whistling and feeds some sandwich crumbs to the pigeons.

'They all claim inspiration from the Holy Spirit, but how can the truth of the Holy Spirit end up with so many different interpretations? There has to be an authority.'

In an act of frustration, Charlie throws a sandwich at a bird sitting near the feet of the preacher. 'The gospels were corrupted by the early church… and that prick of an emperor, whose name I can't remember, changed everything.'

'Really! In that case my good, sir, God's a liar because he promised that not even hell itself would ever destroy His church.

Yes, not even hell… so, what chance did Constantine and any other Romans have?'

Charlie looks at the preacher, pitying him standing in the sweltering heat.

'My friend, believe me, I don't wish to convert you to any religion. You must find divine truth yourself. But on your journey, seek forgiveness, because sin will continue to separate you from Almighty God.'

'Don't talk to me about sin. We are all bloody sinners, even you!'

'Correct! But did you know that even the great Protestant reformer Martin Luther added the sacrament of confession to his new church because, as he said, confession is a singular medicine for afflicted consciences.'

Charlie is now lying stretched out on the lawn looking up at the sky with his ears blocked.

The preacher points his index finger in the air. 'You need authority, sir, and that applies to all walks of life, including the place where you work, and the religion started by Jesus Christ.'

Charlie starts snoring loudly before gathering his belongings. Passers-by look on with smiles or embarrassment.

'The church He created, dear fellow, is not a denomination… it's not one of many… because it is one, holy and apostolic… never a denomination!'

George gets up, shakes the grass off his trousers, giving his bottom a final poultry-like shake, before walking briskly away. He hears the preacher intoning gravely, 'You are a proud man, sir, a proud man going blind with sin and ignorance. Accept the providence of God and rejoice.'

Charlie throws up his arms in despair and quickly crosses West Street before entering the main entrance to the General Post Office.

'Did you enjoy your lunch, Mr. Blignaut?' asks a young clerk.

Swallowing hard, he replies, 'Yeah, until that idiot Bible puncher came along and gave me instant indigestion and constipation.'

'I saw him one evening standing at the bus shelter across the road next to the Salvation Army Band,' the young fellow says with a smile.

'I hope they gave him a loud trumpeting to shut him up,' replies Charlie, shaking his head.

'The Salvation Army does a damn fine job feeding hungry folk,' the chap replies.

Charlie is pleased when 4.30 comes around, so he can peddle his way back to his beachfront flat. He is inclined to give a passing city policeman that he sees walking along the pavement an inverted victory sign, but thinks better of it, and, instead, gives him a middle-finger wave.

The policeman scowls.

On arriving home, Charlie carries his bicycle up one flight of stairs to his one-bedroom bachelor flat, all the time talking away to his old Chooks. His next-door neighbour, Buddy Jones, thinks he is loony and forbids his wife to talk to him. Charlie has hardly settled down to enjoy a cold pint of lager when there is a knock at the front door.

'Oh, it's you, George, come on in my boy.'

Charlie is fond of George and has occasional thoughts of him being a stepson, provided he can persuade his mother to marry him.

'Sorry to disturb you, Charlie, but I'm wanting to find where this Buster fellow lives.'

'Buster?' Charlie doesn't initially register. 'Oh, you mean the guy who entertained Susan. Of course, yes, yes, you need to get some answers from that blighter.'

'He apparently has a flat somewhere along the beachfront.'

'He won't be easy to find because there are hundreds of flats along here. Do you have any idea what he looks like?'

The very mention of Buster is enough to stir emotions of vengeance in George.

'My advice, my lad,' says Charlie, 'is to go to the supervisor of each block and ask.'

George, who is still standing outside in the windy passageway, asks, 'Can I come in for a minute?'

'Yes, yes, sorry... come on in, my boy.'

Charlie offers George a beer, which he gratefully accepts and the two engage in a conversation about Susan and the tragic consequences of her meeting with this dubious fellow, Buster. George punches his open hand. 'As far as I'm concerned, this guy's dead meat!'

'Steady on there, George, don't rush to conclusions.'

George takes comfort in the chilled beer while Charlie offers him a savoury snack.

'If I can talk to you man-to-man...' George pauses briefly before continuing. 'You know, the truth of my relationship with Susan...' He again pauses before marshalling his thoughts. 'I could never make her happy. I could give her pleasure sometimes, and we could laugh and enjoy things together, but then it would all evaporate leaving behind emptiness. I could see that she was not a happy person.'

'But, did she make you happy?'

George reflects for a moment before replying. 'No, not really! As I said, she gave me pleasure and sometimes a good meal. But we often had to rely on booze to feel bonded, as if other stuff in her life had to be forgotten.'

'Did you make the right choice in marrying her?'

'What I soon learned about marriage is that great sex and high hopes soon fade, and one is left with the challenge of having to make it work, especially for the sake of Candice.'

Charlie chooses his words carefully saying, 'Was she a faithful wife?'

'If you mean like a pet, no! She liked her independence.' Inwardly, George is wracked in doubt about Susan's fidelity and he takes another swig of the refreshing lager before adding, 'Susan was a very pretty woman. Men admired her... and she was a bit of a flirt. But if she ever went to bed with another man, I can't answer that for sure.' He bites his lip recalling recent events, 'But if that Buster fellow tried anything, I want to know.'

Charlie notices that George's beer glass is nearly empty and gets up to offer another one.

'No, thanks Charlie, I must be getting back. Bessie is playing mother to Candice tonight, and I've got to get her bathed and into bed.'

Wanting to meet Buster now becomes an overpowering obsession, and the following evening George visits a popular ladies' bar along North Beach, taking a seat against the long bar counter. He soon gets chatting to the chap next to him, asking, 'By the way, do you know a guy called Buster?'

The chap shakes his head.

George stands up and announces loudly, 'I need to get hold of a good electrician by the name of Buster. Anybody know of him?'

The fellow next to him comments, 'You sound desperate. I can recommend a good sparky called Anthony.'

No one in the bar responds to the name Buster, but George receives several other names of highly recommended electricians, one of which approaches him.

'Hi, my name's Jack Pearson. Can I assist?'

'Have you heard of a chap called Buster?'

The fellow laughs, 'Ja, I've heard of him,' and turns to those around him to share in his joke, 'I sure have... Buster Keaton.'

George prepares to leave the bar as he hates being made fun of when he is deadly serious.

'Hang on there, old chap,' says Pearson.

Pearson is a middle-aged electrician with a developing lager girth. 'I'm an electrician. That's my trade?'

George feels embarrassed about his open announcement but is unapologetic as he is determined to find the man who could provide answers to Susan's suicide.

'Thank you... have you a business card?'

'No, but I'll write my phone number on this.' He takes a menu from the table next to him and jots down his contact details. 'By the way, that name does ring a bell. Yeah, I think Buster Evans is the man you may be looking for, but... but, if that is the guy, he hasn't a good name in the trade so I wouldn't recommend him.'

'Do you know where he stays?'

With that pointed question, Pearson assumes that George

wants the man for more than his electrical skills and looks at him suspiciously. 'No, sorry, but I believe he plays rugby for some or other club.'

'Thanks... much appreciated.'

George becomes increasingly obsessed with the notion that this fellow Buster was somehow involved in Susan's death, and to find him is now a quest that he is not easily going to give up.

Chapter 7

The Pie Cart

The eastern pavement flanking Smith Street opposite the city hall, where most of the city's cinemas are located, comes alive on Friday and Saturday evenings with moviegoers in quest of entertaining escapism. The nearby hotel bars of the Royal, the Mayfair, the Broadway and the Waverley are popular drinking holes for local whites wanting to gear their minds for a good time, and it is on the veranda of the Waverley Hotel where Buster and his pal, Jimmy Wallis are sitting, hoping to attract passing female company.

Now, just after 5.30, they decide to catch the early show at the 20th century cinema of *The Longest Day,* a gripping wartime movie on the Normandy landing of June 1944. Buster tries his luck with an attractive woman he sees in the foyer, but she promptly gives him the brush-off.

After the movie, he and Jimmy return to the Waverley to continue drinking until Jimmy leaves shortly before 11 pm to catch the last Umbilo bus home. Buster decides to walk back to his beachfront flat via nearby Pine Street, stopping on the way at the all-night pie cart to have a snack. While eating a hot dog, a tall man in a long black cloak and hat sidles up to him.

'Evening, good fellow.'

Buster glances up but doesn't wish to engage in conversation, so he simply nods his head and turns away.

'A God-given evening to you,' the persistent stranger says.

'Ja, whatever you like.'

The man orders a cup of coffee and sandwich, and, when he pays, Buster notices his bulging wallet. This immediately piques his interest, and he opens a conversation. 'Have you been to the movies?' not caring whether the stranger had spent the evening on the moon.

'No, sir, I have been doing the Lord's work, tilling His vineyard, so to speak.'

'What sort of tilling is that? Shovelling shit between the vines, or thrusting religion down peoples' throats?'

The stranger appears immune to insults. 'I try to show people a better way to live.'

'Isn't that a thankless job?'

The man gives Buster a searching smile. 'What does life mean to you, sir?'

'A pint of beer and a good *skrop*.'

'Sorry, what does that word mean? I'm from England and unfamiliar with your local slang'

'It means a good fuck.'

'Does that bring you peace and happiness?'

'No, but it guarantees a great cock stand and a good night's kip.'

'Is that all that life means to you?'

'Why? Is there more?'

'Have you ever asked yourself, why you are here?'

'I'm here because I'm fucking hungry and pissed and need to sober up for the walk back home.'

'But what is your real purpose on this earth?'

'What purpose? It's a dog eat dog world... and that's that.'

'What if I told you that God's plan for your life has yet to be fulfilled?'

'I'd say, piss off!'

Buster mentally sums up the man's physical abilities, dismissing his slight height advantage as he considers himself to be much stronger and younger. Not only does Buster keep reasonably fit by playing rugby, he periodically goes to the gym when he's not drunk and debauched. The tall man in black produces a Bible from his jacket pocket, saying, 'You don't appear to be the sort of man who likes to talk about religion.'

'I hate religion. All the religious people I know are bloody hypocrites... always ready to condemn the things we do... but do the same things behind our backs.'

He puts the Bible back in his pocket, turns to Buster, saying, 'You're right... we are all sinners.'

'So that's it! Let's talk about sex then,' chirps Buster, thinking he has stumped the preacher.

'Okay! Say now you allow your concupiscence to override your good judgment and you have sex with a woman and she falls pregnant. What's your response?'

'Abort the little shit, what else?'

'So, you think that the principle of freedom... your freedom to end a human life tops the principle of life?'

'Why not? Freedom tops the lot.'

'So, you believe that if I am an obstacle to your freedom, you are entitled to take my life?'

'Why not?'

'And if the boot were on the other foot, and you were an obstacle to my freedom?'

'Just try!' Buster replies threateningly.

'The principle of life must always top the freedom of choice.'

Buster spits out a piece of sinew, 'So, what's that got to do with the price of eggs?'

'There's a fundamental principle involved in what you or anyone else can justifiably do with a living human being... and I emphasize the word, living, even if it's tiny and unborn.'

Buster looks at him scathingly. 'Just eat your fucking sandwich and talk about the real world.'

'Think about it... if your presence were an inconvenience to me, would I have the right to take your life?'

'Look, are you threatening me?'

The tall fellow gives up, deciding to quietly finish his sandwich, as everything he says is falling on deaf and defiant ears. He turns his attention to the man sitting on his opposite side, 'Excuse me sir, do you realize that you have a Creator who takes a keen interest in what you do, even though you may not realize it.'

The man ignores the comment, but Buster responds, saying with a mouth full of chips, 'Are you trying to tell me that God loves someone like me?'

'Next time you look in the mirror, sir, check your amazing eyes... even if they're bloodshot from heavy drinking, they will clear. Check your body's ability to do everyday chores as well as some extraordinary things. You are an amazing creation... unique and loved by your heavenly Father. Yes, your life is truly amazing! Don't destroy it... or take anybody else's life.'

Buster pretends to be taken in with this view. 'Ja, I suppose, you're right! I couldn't have made myself, because if I did, I would've put in some improvements, like an extra inch or two, if you know what I mean.'

'You're a fine-looking young man... on the outside... but I suspect you have accumulated a lot of rotten stuff that is blocking the beauty that lies within.'

Buster gives him a closer inspection. 'Aren't you the bloke who rants and raves in Farewell Square?'

The preacher seems to take the barbed comment as a compliment. 'Well, my good sir, if you're a street evangelist you have to raise your voice, otherwise, no one will listen to you.'

Buster's mind is scheming on how to get this fellow into a secluded spot and tries to mastermind a ploy.

'Would you pray...' But he doesn't know how to put the question to the preacher, not knowing whether he should be prayed over or with or what.

The preacher senses his desire, even if it is insincere, but is prepared to give him the benefit of the doubt. 'Do you want me to pray with you?'

'Ah, yes,' sighs Buster, finding a way out of his dilemma.

The preacher turns in his seat and raises his hands over Buster, who catches the smirk on the face of the stranger sitting opposite him. He hates being mocked.

'Not here... I'm not used to this sort of thing.'

'In the meantime, can I pay for your dog?'

Buster laughs uproariously and turns to the preacher with a feigned apologetic expression. 'Sorry, I'm a bit pissed...'

The preacher doesn't understand what he's getting at.

'I thought you said, can I pray for your dog... ja, I suppose it needs a prayer before I gobble it up.' Buster opens the roll and says to the Vienna sausage in a funny voice, 'Hey, buddy boy, this good preacher is going to give you a bye-bye prayer,' and then bursts out laughing.

The preacher enjoys the humour and pays for Buster's hot dog and chips as well as for the sandwich and coffee, which he quickly finishes before moving off with Buster in the direction of the nearby railway workshop sheds. They gain access through a side gate and move into the darkness between the huge corrugated structures. Traffic noise muffles a cry from behind one of the sheds. Shortly afterwards, Buster is seen walking rapidly down Pine Street back to his flat.

On the way to work the following morning, George happens to read a *Natal Mercury* billboard, *Street Preacher Found Dead*. He instinctively knows it is the Bible puncher whom he had tried so often to avoid in the past. He buys a copy of the newspaper to read about the deceased who was a defrocked Catholic priest, who had held heretical views on priestly celibacy and divorce that were contrary to canonical teaching. He had been living in England with a divorced woman whom he later married. When the woman died a few years later, he emigrated to South Africa hoping to be rehabilitated into the church and priesthood, but his situation was still under review at the time of his death. The 'mad monk', as George called him, continued to feel a strong compulsion to spread God's word, but his only available pulpit was the street. He drew a monthly income from the proceeds of his late wife's estate and had rented a bedsitter in Smith Street. The final line in the newspaper article mentions that police are investigating, and an appeal is made to anyone with any information about the incident to contact the police. A member of the local Catholic laity has offered to pay for his funeral.

When George arrives at his mother's house that evening to find Candice bathed and fed and sitting on the lounge carpet doing homework, he is painfully aware of how much she still misses her mother, even calling for her on occasion. He cannot suppress a strong compulsion to find the culprit who caused Susan's death, because he cannot accept the suicide verdict. Winnie has made dinner and is sitting near Candice ready to help with her homework. She looks up at George with a smile, 'I thought I'd give your mother a break today.'

Bessie's eyes always brighten in the presence of her son. 'Come through to the kitchen, my boy, and sit down. How was your day?'

'I made further inquiries about that Buster fellow.'

Bessie brushes her hair back with a sweep of the hand. 'Forget him! Nothing can be done, it's all in the past.'

'I want justice for Susan… and I'm more convinced than ever that she didn't commit suicide.'

Slightly agitated, Bessie knocks over her glass of wine. 'What makes you think that?'

'She could have been murdered. Maybe she was going to expose what this bastard was up to. I don't know, but I'm determined to find out.'

Overhearing the conversation, Winnie quickly gets up and closes the kitchen door, but Candice is playing with her farmyard animals and doesn't appear to hear and react.

George strongly believes that Susan would be the last person in the world to take her own life. 'She loved life, and loved herself far too much,' he says to his mother.

'So, what are you suggesting?' Bessie asks with arching eyebrows.

'I'm suggesting that the facts don't add up… there's something I don't know and I'm not going to rest until I find out what it is.'

Bessie reminds George that the death certificate clearly states that it was the result of a self-inflicted overdose, and in her matriarchal manner says sternly, 'This subject must end. Now! Nothing can bring the woman back and Candice doesn't want to have to live with the thought of a mother who died in mysterious circumstances.'

'Rather that than the memory of a mother who took her own life and abandoned her daughter,' George says under his breath, as he leaves the room.

Chapter 8

Hot on the Trail

George is jogging along the northern beachfront early in the morning and pauses briefly to watch a white-chinned petrel dust bathing on a sandy patch in the dunes. The bird is rubbing its plumage against a swarm of tiny, crawling insects, occasionally stopping to pick up some in its bill as if selecting those that it specifically wants to rub on its feathers and skin. The petrel is performing with such precision and persistence that it makes him think of his mother and her obsessive determination in getting things done to a fine degree. He knows that he derives his obsessive nature from her, and it's that compulsion that won't let him shake off wanting to settle things with Buster.

He returns to the ladies' bar in the late afternoon to ask if anyone had seen him. He sees Jack Pearson sitting alone at the bar counter and sidles up to him. Jack gives him a cursory glance, saying blandly, 'Have you found your man?'

'Not yet.'

'I have some information, but I can't guarantee that it's reliable.'

George looks searchingly into the man's eyes.

'I heard that he works for Joe's Electrical.'

George waits eagerly to hear more but Jack averts his gaze. 'That's all I know.'

Pausing momentarily to soak in the information, George

turns his back on the barman, and hurriedly makes his way to a nearby public telephone booth to check out the name of the firm. A female receptionist answers. 'May I speak with Buster?'

'I'm sorry, sir, but Buster Evans has left the company.'

'You mean resigned.'

'No, he didn't resign. He was...'

'Fired?'

'Yes.'

'When was that?'

'Last Friday was his last day here.'

'Do you know where I can contact him? It's a family matter, and quite urgent.'

'I've got his home address here. Just hold on a minute.'

George can hear background voices, and the receptionist saying, 'He's looking for Buster.' An off-phone voice asks, 'Is it the police?'

'No, a family member.'

The receptionist resumes the conversation with George. 'He lives in Arona Court in Playfair Road.'

'Thank you.'

'But you may be wasting your time, as I'm told he was going to Johannesburg to look for work.'

'Was he planning to go by car?'

'I don't know, sir, but I do know that he likes to travel by train.'

'Thank you, you've been most helpful.'

George knows the block of flats and quickly makes his way on foot arriving at the front door without any clear approach, except to confront the man directly. There is no response to his knocking. As he is about to go, the next-door occupant opens his door and says that Buster has gone out, he thinks to the station.

Buster takes the trolley bus into town, then hurriedly makes his way to the nearby railway station, knowing that the daily Trans-Natal Express leaves at 6 pm. It's now just after five and he moves to the main platform to ask the Ticket Examiner, who is holding a long, unfurled scroll of names and compartment details of those travelling on the overnight express.

'Excuse me,' he asks in an agitated tone. 'Is a Mr. Buster Evans on your list?'

The middle-aged Afrikaner, dressed in his smart black uniform and peaked cap, checks the list but finds no Buster Evans. George then hurries across to the main ticket office to make inquiries about those travelling the following day.

'Yes, we have a Mr. Buster Evans booked in a second-class coupe.'

George is presented with a strategy.

'Are you wanting to share the coupe? There's a spare bunk.'

George immediately replies, 'yes, yes.' But not having given the matter any serious thought, he books purely on impulse.

The following morning, he tells the manager of the car lot where he works that an urgent family matter has arisen and that he needs to travel to Johannesburg, hoping to return two days later. He tells his mother that he is being sent to Johannesburg to pick up a vehicle.

With a string of lies and deception to cover his absence, he boards the train and finds the allocated compartment. No sign of Buster until five minutes to six when a burly individual enters the compartment heavily under the influence. George feels a sudden bloodlust to kill the drunken brute and stretches out a clenched right hand, but then relaxes his fingers to shake Buster's sweaty paw. 'I'm Pete.'

'Hi, I'm Buster.'

Buster shoves his suitcase in the rack above the top bunk, cussing as he does so. 'The barman at the railway bar was so fucking slow I couldn't get in my last order.' He takes a packet of plain Texan toasted cigarettes from his jacket pocket, flips one out, lights it, and flops into the seat by the window. George scrutinizes his rugged countenance and sees why some women like Susan could find him attractive. Despite an overwhelming hatred of the man, George is beginning to enjoy the aroma of the Texan cigarette but not even that can dispel the rotten presence of the man, and he is finding it difficult to control his emotions. George believes that the best way to conceal his true feelings is to engage in small talk, so he begins to pry. 'Do you live in Joeys... perhaps going back after a holiday?'

'No, I'm going on business.'

'Ja, me too!'

Buster crudely laughs. 'I told my ex-boss to stuff a 15-amp plug up his *poephol* and get some light into his fucking miserable life.'

'So... you're an electrician.'

'Yup! And you?'

'Me?' George quickly concocts an answer with the first thought that enters his head. 'I work at the Post Office just across the road.'

'Sorting letters?'

'A little more exciting than that! I'm an auditing clerk,' believing that to be Charlie's position at the GPO.

'I would never work for this fucking Nat government. Never!' Buster pauses, drawing deeply down on his Texan. 'You sound English-speaking?'

'Yup!'

'Then you can kiss your arse goodbye for any big promotion at the GPO. They all go to the Dutchmen.'

'Not all of them,' although he can't immediately think of any English-speaking person who holds a senior position there.

'If you're not one of the bloody *herrenvolk* you're a fucking nobody.'

'Herrenvolk?'

George's thoughts are miles away from any 19th-century German colonial concept of racial superiority. He wants to get to the nub of the conversation, to ask this chap if he knew Susan but realizes that such a question would not be the best tactic, so he skirts around the subject.

'Are you married?'

'Fuck, no! Why would I want to screw up my life with a wife and screaming brats?'

'Are you leaving a girlfriend behind?'

He utters a dismissive guffaw. 'Joburg's full of hot chicks, so I leave behind no lovesick Sheila.'

His contempt for women galls George, suggesting that he would have had scant respect for Susan, whom he had used purely to gratify his lustful desires. George ponders, how does he get this guy to open up about his relationship with her? Perhaps he likes to brag about his many conquests and exploits.

Meanwhile, Buster scrounges around in his jacket pockets for another cigarette and accidentally pulls out a pamphlet, which he tosses aside. The front-page title, *Sacrifice,* catches George's attention and he begins to read something about the Aztec civilization.

'I forgot to throw this shit away,' and tries to snatch it back from George, who starts reading it. 'Hey, check this! It says that the Aztecs of Mexico used to sacrifice their children to the sun god.'

'Ag, man, it's a load of crap.' Buster pauses briefly. 'I got it from some crazy Bible puncher at the pie cart. He was trying to explain to me some crap about the importance of sacrifice. Can you imagine me wanting to sacrifice anything… other than a woman who pisses me off?' His face turns mean. 'Most women piss me off!'

'Anyone in particular?' asks George, with his blood pressure peaking.

'No, but when a woman pisses me off, she must fuck off.'

George reads other layers of meaning into his comments that strike closer to home. He thinks this article may be a way to get Buster to make unguarded comments. 'It says here that the Aztecs used to sacrifice their children to their gods. Crazy, hey!'

'Stupid arseholes!'

'Apparently, they had a whole bunch of gods to feed. They liked to sink their teeth into raw baby bums. They had this sun god to keep happy and to make sure that the old bugger showed up every day… and then the rain gods had to be satisfied otherwise they would send terrible storms and droughts.'

George continues with forced laughter before picking up on another line in the hope that it will goad Buster into talking about the killing of people. 'It says here that people, men, and women, were murdered... except they called it a sacrifice. They'd chop off their heads, pull out their hearts while they were still alive...'

'Hey, man, go easy on that stuff. Do you want me to puke?'

'Who did you say gave you this pamphlet?'

'Did you ever see that mad prick all dressed in black, menacing the good folk in Farewell Square?'

'Ja, I've seen him, but always managed to avoid him, but a friend of mine told me that he doesn't let up.'

George passes his brandy flask to Buster, hoping to intoxicate him even further, and utters another forced guffaw. 'Hey, listen to this. It says that sacrifice is something we all need to do. Abraham was prepared to sacrifice his son Isaac, and that God sacrificed his Son, Jesus.'

'Yeah, yeah, I think I've heard all that crap before.'

Tossing the pamphlet aside, George replies with a hollow laugh, 'Who the hell am I supposed to sacrifice?'

'Someone should have told that prick that parents sacrifice their sons every time there's a bloody war. If I had ever met him on Farewell Square, I would've pointed to the nearby Cenotaph and said, check there you big poes, there's a fucking monument to sacrifice!'

'Sure thing!'

'Hey, all this talk of sacrifice is making me hungry.'

The mail train picks up speed as it moves into the countryside outside Durban, and a soft, sunset haze hangs over the crimson horizon. Buster shouts at the setting sun. 'Hey, make sure you pitch up for work tomorrow, otherwise no more sacrifices for you, sunny boy.' He turns to George with a smile, 'You can never rely on anything these days.'

Buster's drooping eyelids appear to succumb to the rhythmic click-clack of the steel wheels passing over the tracks. George looks at him with an abiding hatred, and if he had a knife he would've plunged it deep into the man's heart, cutting the detestable thing from his chest and throwing it into the nearest toilet. But the thought of being hanged for his murder only adds to his anguish and he fervently hopes to find another way. About half an hour later, the train hits something big, the impact and accompanying high-pitched squealing of the steel brakes jolts Buster awake. 'What the fuck!' he cries out.

It's too dark outside to see what could have caused the incident, but within minutes the train starts moving forward slowly. Looking out the window George sees the carcass of an ox lying on the side of the track. 'Poor bugger must have strayed onto the line.'

'Ja, and sacrificed its miserable life for our sake,' Buster guffaws. 'So, let's go and drink to the dead beast!'

Buster is on his feet and looks to George to join him. The train picks up speed as they gently sway their way along the narrow corridor to the saloon, occasionally gripping the chrome hand railing for balance. The white Afrikaans-speaking barman greets them and takes their order for two cold Castle lagers. Perched on a barstool, George is momentarily nostalgic about the time when he and Susan had taken the Trans-Natal express to Pretoria to visit her parents. They, too, had sat at the bar before going into the dining saloon for dinner, a simple event that now assumes significance.

George takes his time drinking his beer, as he wants to maintain his sobriety, while Buster is happy to keep drinking to the base of his boots and downs another two lagers before they go into the dining saloon where he orders a bottle of red wine. The conversation is reduced to Buster looking lustily at several young women sitting nearby, and making muted, crass comments about the size of their boobs. But what shocks George is when he comments on a young man sitting across the aisle. 'Check that handsome fucker!' he says, with glistening eyes. 'I could take him down a peg or two,' and leaning across the starched linen tablecloth, adds conspiratorially, 'ja, from the back into the back.' He guffaws and raises his glass in a toast. 'Have you ever fucked a woman's arse?'

George quickly looks across to the opposite table in the hope that no one overheard him.

'As a sparky, I regard it as the tradesman's preferred entrance and very close to the fuse box.'

Dribbling beer from the corner of his mouth, he whispers, 'It's such a tight fit that my cock is locked in glory-land before it comes.'

George is repulsed while Buster's mind slips into recent reminiscences, 'I had one chick,' he snorts. 'Shit! She was bloody pretty. I took her to my flat to screw her arse off, but she didn't want to let me in through the tradesman's entrance, so I gave her a taste of her own crap.'

'What do you mean?' asks George, who is by this time feeling so enraged that he has to physically restrain himself.

'I shoved my cock into her mouth.'

George feels sick to the pit of his stomach and holds the serviette to his mouth.

'Who was this woman?'

'Why, do you also want a turn?' Buster guffaws.

George cannot stand to even look at the man a moment longer and drops his gaze.

'I think her name was Susan. Ja, Suzie Poozie with a sweet tarty farty arse.'

George pukes into the serviette.

'What's up buddy? Not like the beef?'

George says nothing but gets up from the table refusing the offer of dessert and hurriedly makes his way back to the compartment. He is now blind with rage and feels he can no longer control his emotions. He decides to wait outside in the corridor for Buster to return. The 'bedding boy,' as white passengers often refer to these Coloured railway employees, who are often middle-aged men, arrives to make up their bunk beds. George instructs him to make the lower and the top bunks, leaving the middle bunk empty to allow more space for the person sleeping below. The attendant has just left the compartment when Buster is seen staggering along the corridor holding onto the railing for support. On seeing George, he says, 'Hey, Pete, I'm as pissed as an arty fart,' and makes his way directly to the toilet at the end of the coach. George follows him and opens the outside carriage door, which is directly opposite the toilet. He fastens the door to the carriage latch and waits for Buster to emerge from inside.

'Ah, that's a bloody good idea!' says Buster, emerging from the toilet zipping up his fly and vigorously waving his hand in front of his nose. 'Phew! That was a bloody smelly crap! I need some fresh air.'

He gives George a strange leery look. 'I never told you this, Pete, but I spent three years in a reformatory for... you know, doing what I shouldn't have... but every Saturday night, my mate Boet de Jager and I had a special arrangement. You know, boys' night out,' and he giggles. 'Except for us it was boys' night in,' and crudely laughs. The swaying movement of the coach adds to Buster's unsteadiness and he stumbles up against George grabbing his crotch. George retaliates by taking Buster by the collar and pushes him to the edge of the open doorway. Then with a mighty shove, he attempts to throw him off the moving train, but Buster grabs hold of George's shirt and they both go flying out of the open doorway, landing on the hard, stony ground alongside the track. Nobody sees what has happened, and the train continues its journey. Buster is lying groaning in pain on the ground as he took the full brunt of the fall with George landing on top of him. 'My back... shit, my back,' he groans. Buster is barely conscious and bleeding profusely from a large head gash.

'What the fuck did you do that for?' he moans in agony.

'You raped my wife, you bastard!'

'Your wife! Who's your fucking wife?'

'Susan.'

'Susan?'

'Susan Cooksley.'

Buster is stunned silent.

'And you... oh, shit!

'Yes, oh, shit! I'm her husband... you bloody, filthy bastard!

Buster grimaces in pain. 'This is your revenge... is that it?' He struggles to get the words out with his throat beginning to choke in blood.

'Did you follow her to her house after she left your flat, and shove sleeping tablets down her throat?'

'I don't know what... oh, shit, the pain!' With a mighty effort to breathe, he splutters, 'What are you're talking about?'

'Did you kill my wife?'

'No, why would I want to do that?' Buster's voice is weakening with blood pouring from his mouth and gaping head injury.

'I never saw her again after she left...' he gasps. He inhales painfully. 'She left my flat... I swear.'

George looks with contempt at Buster's pathetic, contorted figure lying on the side of the track in agony.

'I swear I never killed her... but...' Buster utters with strenuous effort and reaches out to clutch George's arm. He cries out pathetically, 'Stay with me... don't leave me here to die. Please.'

George shoves Buster's hand away, stands up, seething with hatred for this man, and limps away, his trousers torn, his legs badly bruised, his chest sore and his right arm bleeding from a nasty gash.

'Help me, man. Don't leave me...' he hears from behind.

George swings around saying bitterly, 'What makes you think you're worth saving?

'I can't die with you believing a lie.'

'A lie!'

'I'm human! Yes, human... and I have a fucking con...' He struggles to finish the word, 'conscience.'

George scoffs at the thought. 'You don't have a conscience. You're a fucking animal... worse than an animal.'

'I didn't kill your wife, but I did... '

'Did what?' George glares down at Buster. 'Did what? Tell me you bastard, or I'll crush your head with this rock and let you die like a dog out here.'

'I did kill someone.'

'Who?'

'That... that mad preacher...'

George throws up his arms in dismissal and starts walking away.

'No, wait! Let me explain.'

But Buster's pathetic cries fall on deaf ears as George casts a backward glance spitting out the words, 'Go to hell, miserable shithouse! You're a sacrifice... yeah, a fucking sacrifice to the devil,' and utters a lingering vicious laugh.

Buster's fading voice is cracking, yet barely audible. 'Your wife's a whore... an escort whore. Did you know that?'

George shouts back with intense anger. 'Die bastard! Die!'

'I fucked your wife,' Buster utters in a voice faintly audible, stuttering his dying words with a cursed smile, 'Yes, she's a fucking whore...' his voice chocking in blood, his life fading rapidly on those damning words.

George pauses briefly before continuing to limp towards Ladysmith, about a kilometre away, where he summons help from the stationmaster, who calls an ambulance that is sent out to fetch Buster.

George is dropped off at the local hospital where the matron summons a police officer after she hears that Buster is likely to be lying dead next to the railway tracks. George makes a carefully considered statement to the officer, telling him that he and Buster got drunk and were playing a silly, rough game in the corridor when his companion opened the outside door of the carriage while the train was in motion, saying he was hot. He stood on the top step of the outside carriage with his arms outstretched to cool off. George scrutinizes the expression of the policeman who is taking all this down. 'I tried to pull him back inside, but he lost his balance and fell... pulling me out with him.'

He again looks at the police officer to see whether his story is making a convincing impression. 'It was a terrible accident, believe me.'

Chapter 9

Intrigue

For George to be holed up in Ladysmith for a fortnight is proving to be extremely inconvenient, but the police have to be satisfied that Buster's death was, in fact, an accident and not the result of foul play. George is feeling under siege, which is neither surprising nor incompatible with the history of this town when residents were held under siege by a Boer force for 118 days during the early stages of the Anglo Boer War.

After five days, George is discharged from hospital and is instructed to report to the local police station where he is told that he must remain in the Ladysmith magisterial district until after the post-mortem results are known. 'The deceased had a twin brother in Durban who was unable to travel up here to identify the body, so he sent a female companion who knew the man well and gave us an affidavit.' The police officer shakes his head. 'He was a strong healthy young man. Such a pity!'

When George phones his mother in Durban, she is alarmed to hear of his escapade, which has already reached the press. Charlie Blignaut informed her that George had been pursuing Buster, believing that he was somehow involved in Susan's death. George's boss is also concerned about the suspicious details attached to the alleged accident and has placed him on suspension. George ponders his future and sees doors closing on him, giving rise to concern about Candice's future. Although Bessie is in a position to feed, clothe and house her, this is not a long-term solution.

A police officer calls round at the boarding house where George is staying, to inform him that the post-mortem results show that Buster's fatal injuries were the result of severe blunt trauma to the back of his head – presumably caused by his fall from the moving train. Furthermore, he is told that although there is nothing at this stage to suggest foul play, the investigation is continuing.

'So, we'd like you to look over the statement you gave shortly after the incident, as this will be held in evidence should the case end up in court.'

Trying to calm his nerves, George jokingly says, 'We were drunk and playing silly buggers.'

The officer maintains a stoic expression.

George reads the section where he is quoted as saying that after Buster opened the door he stepped onto the top step of the carriage.

'Yes, that is what happened.'

'And you say, that he opened his arms wide to cool off?'

'Yes, he was holding onto the outside carriage railing with one hand initially, then he released that hand and stretched out both arms shouting something like cool me down, baby.'

'And then you claim he slipped... or, deliberately jumped...?'

'I could see what he was doing was highly dangerous and called out to him to come back inside the carriage.'

'Then, what happened?'

'I stretched out my right arm and grabbed hold of his shirt. But he was so drunk that he took hold of my arm and pulled me outside.'

'And then?'

'He lost his balance and began falling backwards while grabbing onto my arm at the same time.'

The officer writes down all these additional details before saying, 'The case is not officially closed until the prosecutor is satisfied that there is nothing to implicate you in the intentional cause of his death.'

George hides his twitching hands under the table. 'So, am I free to go?'

'For now, yes, but you'll be required to report to your nearest police station when you return to Durban. We have checked on the address you have given us, and it appears to be genuine.'

George is relieved that the police have not managed to uncover the full circumstances of the incident and that there were no witnesses.

Late that evening, he boards the Trans-Natal Express, arriving back in Durban the following morning. Bessie is frantic with worry when she sees him and treats him like an errant teenager, which he strongly resents.

'Just get off my back, okay!'

'I'm just trying to get you out of the mess you've made.'

'It's fine. Everything is fine. There's nothing to worry about.'

'You're going the same way as that no-good drunken father of yours.'

George refuses to listen to anymore and asks where Candice is.

'Well, you can fetch her from nursery school yourself today. I'm always the skivvy when you or that...' She quickly tempers her words, 'or Susan, yes, Susan, who was always gallivanting about the place couldn't fetch her.'

Bessie turns to take the coffee pot off the stove. Her right hand is shaking slightly.

George notices this and retorts, 'Are *you* not perhaps drinking too much?'

She spins around spitting mad. 'How dare you talk to your mother like that!'

George picks up his jacket and storms out through the front door.

Candice is delighted to have her father back home, and George feels a renewed responsibility and bond that he intends to develop with her. He buys two hamburger takeaways for their supper, refusing to return to his mother's home until he can reassess his future, which might even mean making the move that Susan had urged him to do.

He strongly believes the time is ripe to start his own business and visits the Trust Bank the following morning to secure a business loan. He uses his life insurance policy as collateral to secure a small loan, which enables him to buy into a secondhand car dealership in Point Road, whose aged owner wants to retire.

To grow the business, he poaches some of the contacts he made during his previous job, and when this reaches the ears of his former boss, Basil Edwards, he is threatened with court action as George had signed a restraint of trade agreement when joining that firm. However, George maintains that the agreement is invalid as it was signed when he joined the company under a different owner.

George is proud to be growing his new company's profits and within three months has gained a reputation as a reliable and trustworthy dealer. Although no court challenge is immediately forthcoming, Edwards maintains that when he bought the business, all previous legal contracts and agreements made in good faith were still binding. George, however, is concerned that some of his earlier customers are no longer calling on him and hears via the grapevine that Edwards is foul mouthing him, saying that he was responsible for Buster's death.

Meanwhile, Derek visits his brother's North Beach flat to remove furniture and personal belongings and among the items is Buster's appointment book. Derek is intrigued to see how many female customers he had, and takes note of their names and addresses, hoping that he can induce some of them to be part of his widening circle of escort hostesses. One name and telephone number he finds familiar is Susan's, and unaware that she had died, dials her number. He normally only does this after 9 o'clock knowing that her husband would be at work. But this time, George is at home to answer the call.

'Hi, may I speak to Susan?'

'Who's speaking?'

'It's... er... Derek, a friend of a friend,' he utters with an embarrassed laugh.

'A friend of a friend?'

'Ja, I'm Buster's brother and want to tell Susan about what happened to him.'

George's blood runs cold and his mind whirls into a state of vengeful anger, but, with effort, he forces a bland response. 'Oh...'

'Yes, I was just following up on his customers' contact book to inform her... and others of his death... and that I could recommend a reliable alternative electrician.'

George decides to play along.

'I'm sorry to hear this,' he says, gritting his teeth. 'How did he die?'

George detects hesitation in Derek's voice, 'Oh, did you not read about it in the newspaper?'

'Ah, there's so much junk in the papers, I don't read every story.'

'Ja, he... got into a fight with some bloke on the train to Joburg and fell out the carriage.'

'So, it was an accident?'

'Yeah, as far as we know, but I'm not so sure. Someone was travelling with him, and I want to get hold of that bugger to ask him some probing questions because my brother was tough and wouldn't just fall out of a moving train.'

There is silence from George.

''Anyway, I don't want to bother you with the details, but I think there was more to this than meets the eye if you know what I mean?'

'Yeah, sure.'

'So, is Susan not available?'

'Er... she left to go back home to stay with her parents... somewhere in the Transvaal.'

'Are you related?'

'No... I've taken over the lease.'

'Well, in that case, I'm sorry to have bothered you, but if you need any electrical jobs done, call me back. The name's Derek and my telephone number is 51-1034.'

George puts down the receiver, wondering about the secret life Susan led before her death. Would other men be phoning for her as well? His attention is distracted by Candice playing with her favourite Shirley Temple doll that Bessie had given her for Christmas, causing him to feel wretched and resentful that his child is left without the nurturing care of a mother.

Leaving Buster to die on the side of a railway track gives him no lasting satisfaction, although he retains a strong sense that he was somehow implicated in her untimely death. He lifts Candice into his arms, cradles her tightly and kisses her tenderly. He later retires to the lounge to relax with a cold beer before preparing the evening meal, suppressing a raft of thoughts that Susan had been involved in many adulterous and dubious activities.

Chapter 10

Unexpected Encounter

When George calls round at his mother's place, he finds his aunt Winnie dressed in her nurse's uniform standing in the kitchen preparing to put a cake in the oven. With no family birthday coming up he can't think of any reason for the occasion, as cake baking is not something that happens often in his mother's home. When commenting on the pleasant vanilla aroma he is told that Charlie is coming for tea, giving rise to unspoken speculation that Winnie is counting on a gastronomic approach to win his heart, as all previous attempts have failed. George knows full well that Charlie is romantically interested in his mother, who in turn, spurns his advances, so the only way for Winnie to get Charlie to come within her ambit is to invite him to Bessie's house. The irrepressible Bessie is sitting in the lounge smoking a cigarette, anxious to know whether George has fully recovered from his ordeal.

'That was a dreadful business, my son!'

George doesn't respond.

'Who was this Buster fellow? I saw his picture in the paper and...'

George gives her a long, searching look.

'Guess!'

'He looks like the electrician fellow who called round at your house.'

'Yeah! That's him! I didn't know the chap until I met him on the train.'

Bessie finds that incredible. 'Really!'

'Okay, okay, I tracked the bastard down.'

'So, you killed him?'

'No! He was blind drunk and aggressive. I tried to save him from falling...'

'Save him! Come now George, you can't pull the wool over my eyes.'

'We had a fight, but... but the bugger pulled me off the train with his fall.'

Winnie comes through to the lounge and pumps up the cushions on the couch.

Bessie deliberately plays down the incident on the train. 'Oh, well, my son, you mustn't let that bother you now. At least you're safe and that's all that matters... for the sake of Candice.'

A knock at the front door has Winnie patting down her permed hair that she coloured brunette. She quickly unties the apron strings and beckons to Bessie to let Charlie in. It's not Charlie, however, but Sergeant Lotter from the local Police Station.

'Good afternoon! I'm looking for Mr. George Cooksley.'

Bessie wants to reply that he is not here, but George steps forward.

'I called at your residence next door where the maid told me you might be here.'

'So, what's the problem?'

'You have been charged with culpable homicide for the death of Buster Evans.'

'What!'

'That's nonsense!' cries Bessie. 'He was attacked by that drunken maniac, who caused his own death, and nearly that of my son.'

'You can tell that to the judge. But, in the meantime, I need you to come to the police station and make a further statement.'

'What's wrong with the one I gave in Ladysmith.'

'That was before the post-mortem.'

'They told me in Ladysmith that there was nothing in the post-mortem to suggest any wrong deed.'

'There were signs of a physical struggle.'

'Are you placing me under arrest?'

'Only if you resist.'

George braces himself and is led out of the house.

He looks back at Winnie, 'Save me a slice for later, aunty Win.'

'Leave my son alone! He's a good man. He has a young daughter to look after.'

'Sorry, madam, I'm just doing my duty.'

A fellow policeman is waiting outside the front door and George is escorted to the nearby Point Police Station. Bessie stands in the open doorway howling expletives as her son is led away.

'I'm not going to let them take him away,' she blurts out and follows the policemen escorting George.

Winnie, in a state of shock, sinks deep into the couch and lights a cigarette, unaware that the front door has been left wide open and Charlie walks inside unnoticed. He stands over her with a broad smile. Sitting up in surprise, Winnie declares, 'Oh, it's you!'

'Is it Open Day today?'

Feeling ruffled and surprised, she replies, 'Open! Open for what?'

'The door was wide open, are you welcoming all and sundry?'

'No, no! Bessie's gone with George to the police station to sort out some personal business.'

She gets up to close the door, and while passing the lounge mirror she quickly puckers her lips and puts on a pouty smile.

'Now, Mr. Charlie Blignaut, you just take a seat while I'll make you a nice cup of tea.'

'Ta, very much, Win, but I'd prefer a cup of coffee.'

She gives him a wink, 'Can do… you naughty fellow,' and directs him to the couch.

'What sort of business is Bessie sorting out at the police station?'

'Oh, you don't want to know. It's something to do with George.'

'You mean the carry-on we read about in the papers?'

'Something like that! But we're not going to trouble ourselves with those details.' She gives him a winsome smile, 'I've baked a sponge cake.'

'Ah, that's nice!'

'Yes, I knew you'd like that.'

Winnie is soon bustling about the kitchen humming, *Where the Boys Are*.

'I see you're a Connie Francis fan?' he shouts from the lounge.

'I try to keep up with the times. The young nurses at Addington like her songs very much,' she replies, re-entering the lounge with a tray of coffee and cake, which she puts down before him as if it were a libation, then pats her right cheek to cool the blush.

Charlie doesn't often see Winnie in her nurse's uniform that makes her more appealing and attractive. He sugars his coffee curious to know more about the men she has had in her life, beginning with her late husband.

'What was Len like?'

She initially ducks the question. 'I've sugared it. I know how much you take. Anyway, making it a little sweeter won't do you any harm.' She briefly pauses and picks up on the conversation. 'Oh, Len! He was a good man. But he struggled after losing his leg in the battle of Delville Wood. He ended up with a wooden leg.'

Charlie visualizes poor Len battling in bed with a peg leg. 'I suppose he took it off before he got into bed?'

She looks at him curiously.

'Yes, of course.'

Charlie smiles.

'Are you having improper thoughts, Mr. Naughty Blignaut?'

'Not at all!'

'My Len was proud of his army days, but it cost him dearly.'

'And Reg?'

'Oh, my dear, Reg! He's such a washout! Got fired two weeks ago from his job in Durban and is now working up in Pretoria on a construction site as a crane operator.'

She puts a large slice of cake on a side plate for Charlie. 'Now, you be a good boy, and eat all that, not a crumb wasted, you understand.'

She proffers a look of fake concern as if she has good reason to mother him. 'You're looking very gaunt around the gills. You need to put some weight on.'

She sidles up to him on the couch as he edges slowly away. She takes a genteel sip of coffee, sits back and watches him devour the soft spongy cake, momentarily seeing herself being passionately consumed by this eccentric man.

'You're a handsome old sot, Charlie Blignaut. Did anyone ever tell you that?'

Assuming an affected modesty, he replies with a smile, 'Not in such flattering terms, no.'

'I'm glad my sister's not here, because you'll then be paying her all the attention.'

He looks slightly embarrassed as he has a deep affection for Bessie that he doesn't feel for Winnie. But Winnie is not going to lose the opportunity of having Charlie all to herself, and she takes her right index finger to wipe away the cake crumbs from his mouth.

'They make your mouth look quite scrummy.'

'And the rest of me?'

'Well, I like your cologne,' she whispers.

'My what?'

'Whatever you're using under your arms.'

As an aging Lothario, Charlie is unaccustomed to talk about such private matters and believes that she is breaching boundaries. He thinks that she could next be asking if he powdered his crotch. However, he is tempted to give his armpits a quick sniff, as he hadn't noticed any pleasant odours coming from that quarter before, other than stale sweat.

She snuggles up to him, resting her head on his shoulder.

'Aren't you tired of living on your own? Hmmm?'

She leans over him in her nurse's uniform, as if ready to slip in a bedpan should it be urgently needed. 'Aren't you lonely?'

she purrs.

Feeling decisively trapped on a two-seater couch, he replies in a tone of surrender, 'I keep myself busy so there's no time to feel lonely.'

'I think it's time you had a woman in your life.'

Charlie murmurs agreement, but his choice wouldn't be her. She gives him an affectionate peck on the cheek.

'You need someone to pamper you. You need a woman's touch.'

Leaning back against the armrest, he blusters, 'Your cake is lovely, Winnie.'

She gets up and immediately cuts him another big slice. This time she feeds him piece-by-piece, wiping away each crumb from his mouth before sealing it with a smacking kiss.

'Now wasn't that delicious?'

Charlie is being aroused by Winnie's close physical proximity, her sensuous touch and the fragrance of her *No: 4711 eau de cologne* perfume, all contributing to cranking up his nascent libido. He takes Winnie in his arms, gives her a French kiss that he had learnt from a friend, and wonders whether she had laced the cake with rhino horn or some potent aphrodisiac.

'You smell and taste delicious,' he says, trying to act like tough John Wayne in a Hollywood Western.

'And you smell like fresh wood chips.'

'Wood chips!'

She laughs, 'Yes, maybe you're Woody Woodpecker?'

She is longing for another passionate kiss, and coos sweetly, 'Tell your Winnie what you've been up to lately… you naughty little Woodpecker?'

'My pecker hasn't been up to anything.'

'Shame, poor thing,' she replies teasingly.

'I had a Turkish bath at lunchtime.'

'A Turkish bath!'

'Yes, it's the one near the Post Office. They rubbed me down with hammam.'

'What on earth is that?'

'Top secret.'

Winnie smiles brightly. This is the moment she has been waiting for, and she starts unbuttoning her uniform before taking his right hand to her breasts.

'Wow, steady on there, Win! I think I need a stethoscope to go further.'

'These aren't old flapjacks, I'll have you know, but pert little melons. I'm a nurse, so, put your ear to them,' she whispers.

Giving her a goofy glance, he asks, 'Can they talk?'

Poor old Charlie hasn't had sex in three years and never acquired any successful technique in lovemaking, so he is left ill-prepared for what follows, but he quickly forgoes any idea of copying a great Hollywood matinee idol.

'I like you very much Mr. Blignaut.' she whispers.

'Oh, Mrs. Matthews, what will my old Chooks have to say about that? She's very jealous, you know.' he utters with a mock laugh.

'You're a man, aren't you?'

'Sure.'

'Then act like one,' she declares in a demanding matronly voice. And, as if to give him instant sexual correction, she seductively places her right hand on his crotch and gently squeezes his penis as if it were a plastic tomato sauce bottle.

Charlie utters a squeal of delight.

She kisses him again.

Released of all restraint, Charlie stretches Winnie out on the two-seater couch and proceeds with the enthusiasm of an over-excited schoolboy to canoodle her melons that she finds more ticklish than stimulating. In the heat of the foreplay, they roll off the couch onto the floor where he quickly loosens his belt, slips off his slacks and underpants, but then can't decide on which side of her to be on… and quickly changes from side-to-side.

'What on earth are you doing Charlie? Are you trying to pole jump me?'

At that critical moment, the front door is flung open and Bessie enters in a state of heightened anxiety after seeing her son being treated like a common criminal.

'Good God! What's going on in here?' she shrieks.

Charlie springs to his feet quickly hiding his erect pole behind a cushion. He fumbles for his underpants, yanks them on, adjusts his trousers and tugs at the zip so fast that it catches his nob. He grimaces but receives no sympathy from either woman. Winnie buttons up her uniform in double-quick time.

'What are you two up to?'

Looking accusingly at Charlie, she declares, 'Charlie Blignaut! You're a disgrace! If you want that sort of thing, there's Point Road one block down.'

Charlie looks sheepish, his face dropping to the floor.

'And... as for you, sister...'

'I'm nobody's thing, thank you very much,' replies an aggrieved Winnie.

'Then, don't turn my lounge into a whorehouse.'

Bessie opens the curtain and the windows.

'Let's get some fresh air in here.'

'We were just being friendly,' insists Winnie, asserting her dignity while straightening her dress.

'I'm ashamed of you, Charlie Blignaut, coming here while I'm out and getting fresh with my sister. I think you should go now.'

'I came over to see you, Bess.'

'Really! That makes it worse. You're disgusting!'

He takes from his jacket pocket a slab of melting Cadbury fruit and nut chocolate.

'This was meant for you, Bess.'

She looks at the droopy half-melted slab and his trouser zip not fully closed, saying scathingly, 'Go! I don't want it! Dirty old man... Sis! Go!'

Charlie tosses his jacket over his shoulders and slinks out.

Bessie gives Winnie a fierce look. 'And, as for you, Winnie, you should be thoroughly ashamed of yourself!'

Winnie gathers her handbag and moves to the front door.

'You're just jealous because he wasn't showing you any affection.'

'Nonsense! I don't want that man touching me, even if he washed his hands with carbolic soap.'

Winnie slams the front door closed.

Bessie turns on the radio to find relief and catches part of the 6 pm news. *'Members of the Black Sash stood in silence outside the Houses of Parliament today, protesting against the government's General Law Amendment Act, commonly known as the Sabotage Act.'*

Bessie sits in her comfortable lounge chair, lights up a cigarette while thinking that some women play a vital role in life highlighting injustice, but she doesn't consider the ramifications of the Sabotage Act, rather seeing herself as a brave woman delivering justice to her son.

.

Chapter 11

Shady Underworld

Although George has to report daily to the Point Police Station, this has not cramped his lifestyle to any great extent, and on Friday evening he is at the Ladies Bar of the Four Seasons Hotel where he joins Hazel, who happens to be sitting alone at one of the tables. He never liked her when Susan was alive, believing that as a single woman she moved in circles that were not in his wife's best interests. She beckons him to join her, saying in her customary raspy voice, 'I'm waiting for a friend, but she hasn't pitched.'

George orders a cold lager and offers Hazel another glass of white wine, which she readily accepts. She looks at him almost piteously, 'I've read all that stuff in the newspaper...' Unsure of his reaction, she briefly pauses before adding, 'you know... about you and Buster on the train.'

George just shrugs his shoulders, giving Hazel space to continue. 'He was a bad character, I know. I tried to warn Susan about him, but he was such a charmer... and so darn good looking that she couldn't resist him.'

George is keen to extract from Hazel all she knows about Derek.

'Did you ever meet his brother?'

He detects a touch of discomfort in her reply. 'We spoke on the phone once.'

She sips the last drop of her wine. 'He's also an electrician, but that's not all he does. He's worse than Buster...'

George offers her a cigarette and eagerly awaits to hear more. 'He's involved in some shady business.'

'What business is that?'

She takes a deep draw on her ciggie, coughs slightly before uttering in an undertone, 'One hears rumours, so I can't be too sure.'

The waiter arrives with the drinks.

Pouring his beer, George asks with some urgency, 'What rumours?'

She scrunches her nose, 'Ah, that he's involved in some...' She looks around before continuing. 'You know... Point Road is full of them. Go to Smugglers and you'll find plenty of them.'

'Prostitutes?'

'Obviously.'

'What's that got to do with Susan?'

'I think... and this is only my guess, that...'

She pauses, not wanting to say anything to offend George or that may implicate her in the saga and whispers, 'Derek involved Susan in his call girl... or, escort business. He said she'd make more money in a week than in six months serving behind the counter at some big store.'

'But Susan was making money doing marketing research, so why did she need more?'

A deathly silence follows. Hazel stubs out her cigarette. 'She never really worked for any marketing company.'

'You mean, she bloody lied to me?'

Hazel shrugs her shoulders.

George is alarmed to hear this, but before Hazel can elaborate further, she sees her friend Patty approaching their table. George is desperately keen to get another word in, and interjects, 'Was Susan definitely involved in the escort business?'

Hazel looks down, remaining silent. He notices Patty talking to a young man, so he indirectly answers his own question. 'Yeah, it all begins to make sense.'

'The person to speak to is Derek. He would surely know about that,' she replies glancing up at Patty, who is now moving away from the young man. 'But be careful of him, George, he's a dangerous individual.'

George's mind flashes back to the times he would come home after 4 pm to find Susan dressed to the nines and being told that she likes to look good for her marketing job. His imagination is wild with troubling images of Susan on lunch dates with visiting businessmen who have one thing in mind, a couple of cosy hours in a hotel bedroom afterwards.

Hazel's attention is by now fully drawn to her friend who is standing next to her at the table.

'Hi, Hazel, my love!' Patty announces, in her harsh shrill voice overriding the ambient background music. George feels uncomfortable and excuses himself, leaving the two women to enjoy their sundowners.

On Monday morning, he decides to make contact with Derek, but under an assumed name. He takes note of his telephone number and dials, 511034.

'Hello, may I speak with Derek.'

'Hold on.'

Moments later he hears a deep male voice. 'Derek speaking.'

George feels an instant tension and takes a deep breath trying hard to relax.

'Hi, Derek, this is Peter Smith. We haven't met but I heard that you could be looking for business opportunities in the area. I think I can help. Could we meet? I have a proposition to put to you.'

'Business proposition! What are you talking about? What sort of proposition?'

'I've bought into a second-hand car dealership, and I need salesmen, so there's an opportunity for someone like yourself.'

'Sorry, what did you say your name was?'

'Peter Smith, but call me, Pete.'

There's a brief pause on the line.

'Why me?'

'I'm looking around for suitable guys, and I've heard that you'd fit the bill.'

'But I'm quite happy where I am.'

'Yeah, but if you make a change, things could improve for you… big time. At least, hear me out.'

There's a brief pause before Derek replies. 'Okay, where? When?'

'Meet me at Smuggies tomorrow evening, at seven o'clock.'

'How do I identify you?'

'I'll be wearing a bright red shirt.'

The following evening, George takes a leisurely walk down Point Road to the Criterion Hotel, which houses the notorious Smugglers Inn. He takes a seat near the door to the passageway that leads onto the docks where there is a customs booth for visiting sailors, who often frequent the place. Seven o'clock is early for Smuggies as the action only starts much later and goes on until about 3 am.

George orders a lager and watches the patrons arriving. The place is gradually filling up and couples have started dancing, including men with men, some dressed as women, and women with women and no questions asked. Apart from sailors and prostitutes, there are university students and middle-class folk from the suburbs entering the gloomy, atmosphere, all looking for a touch of daring decadence in the twilight zone of the docks. Above the ambient chatter and music, he hears an unfriendly voice, 'Peter... Peter Smith.' He spins round in his chair and looks into a very familiar face that almost shocks him silent. He sees the face of Buster.

'Did I catch you by surprise?'

'Ja, you reminded me of someone else.'

'People often confuse me with my twin brother, but no more, because some scumbag has killed him.'

George swallows hard. Derek takes a seat and immediately orders a brandy and coke.

'We're identical twins and I can't tell you how many times people got confused not knowing who's who. But of course, that will never happen again.' Derek furrows his brow and maliciously sniggers, 'And when I catch the bastard who did it, he's dead meat.'

George drops the pitch of his voice to prevent any recognition from his brief telephone conversation with Derek and is thankful that the newspapers never printed his photograph with the story. 'So, who do you think was responsible?' he replies, trying to keep a firm grip on his voice.

'The bitch's husband, who else!'

George takes refuge in a sip of lager.

Derek's evil-looking eyes narrow as he continues. 'I may have spoken to the fucker on the phone, but the bastard lied saying he was the new tenant.'

Derek gulps a mouthful of brandy and coke and belches unapologetically. 'Ah! That was good!' he exclaims before wiping his twisted mouth.

George doesn't take his eyes off Derek but seeing all the booze being poured down the hatch, he tries to make light of it, 'I suppose we can all do with a little Dutch courage.'

'I don't need any fucking Dutch courage. I swear on my boet's grave that I'll get that swine.'

Derek's attention is momentarily distracted by a strong ambrosial fragrance of cheap perfume as a heavily made-up prostitute doing the cha-cha with her sailor partner moves nearer their table. 'Hello, darling!' she waves to Derek, who responds with a dead smile.

Derek lights a cigarette. 'So, what's this proposition you want to make?'

George notices Derek giving another woman a knowing wink. She is young and attractive and is dancing with an older woman. As they dance past the table, George comments, 'It looks like there isn't a chick in the house that you don't know?'

'If you come here often enough, you'll know all the birds.'

George leans forward and raising his voice above the din of the music says, 'Okay, now about my proposition, I've bought into a secondhand car lot along Point Road, and I'm looking for some great salesmen... a guy like you with the gift of the gab. You fit the bill.' On saying this, he realizes that it would be suicide to have Derek working for him, but he can always retract the offer later as the approach is merely a ruse to fraternize with the chap, win his trust, and to find out the full extent to which Susan had been involved in his nefarious underworld activities. He is also counting on Derek refusing the offer, knowing that it is not as financially rewarding as his current ventures, which gets him access to the homes of young housewives who are often bored and looking for ways to make extra cash. Out of curiosity, he asks, 'What's the basic salary?'

'A basic of R165 a month plus 10% on gross profit.'

'Only 10%! Some guys I know earn at least 20% on gross profit.'

George purposely put the figure low, but adds, 'After you prove yourself... say, after three months, we can negotiate something better.'

Derek excuses himself and makes his way through the crowded dance floor to the gents' toilet, allowing George to absorb the unique surroundings. Minutes pass and a prostitute in her mid-forties sits down next to him. 'Can you buy this lady a drink, handsome?'

A waiter appears from nowhere and takes her order of cane spirits and lemonade.

'Hi, I'm Helen.'

George nods.

After a pause, she asks, 'Well, aren't you going to be a gentleman and tell me your name?'

'Peter... Peter Smith.'

'Oh, Peter! Now that's a nice man's name, Peter,' she purrs.

He sees Derek emerge from the toilet, making his way back to the table when a flamboyant young woman accosts him. Meanwhile, Helen's perfume and attitude are demanding George's full attention. 'So, Peter, what do you do for a living?'

'I sell cars... secondhand ones.'

'Cars! Oh, that's nice! I sometimes feel like a secondhand

car,' she replies in a coarse voice. Then screwing up her heavily made-up face, adds, 'A very used one at that...' but getting no reaction from George, bursts out laughing.

George stifles a yawn, but before he can reorientate his bearings he feels the presence of Derek standing behind him. Helen looks up, greeting him effusively. 'Oh, Derek, my darling boy! Is Peter your friend?'

With a straight face, Derek nods and sits down, passing a small packet to Helen, who is then given a dismissive wave of the hand.

'Well, if you'll excuse me, gentlemen, I have someone to see at the bar,' she mutters apologetically.

George watches her saunter off, not to the bar, but to approach a lonesome sailor.

'Some of these bitches are so fucking irritating,' Derek mutters while lighting up a cigarette.

George looks at him trying to get a clearer understanding of his character and personality. 'Do they proposition you, or do you have a different approach?'

Derek is offended by the question, 'What do you mean different approach? I'm always in control.'

'I mean, if you could choose your chick, wouldn't that be preferable?'

'Is that your approach?'

'Yeah... and yours?'

Derek doesn't bother to reply but calls the waiter to order a hamburger and chips.

'Make it two,' says George.

Derek gives George a penetrating look as if there is something about this guy that he hasn't fully fathomed. 'Is there a babe in your life?'

George shakes his head.

'Well, buddy boy, if you need company, contact me.'

'But... er... prostitutes...' George scrunches his nose. 'I don't want to pick up a dose... you know, gonorrhoea or syphilis.'

'Yeah, me too! That's why I don't use them unless I wear a

Frenchie. But I'm talking about clean chicks… housewives.'

George's blood runs cold. 'Housewives!' he echoes, his pitch dropping half an octave.

'Ja, those who are so fucking bored with their husbands that they'd sell their pussies for fifty bucks.'

Thoughts of Susan flood his mind, and he wants to punch Derek off his chair.

'One thing about my *boet*, he was bloody sharp at winning a chick's confidence, but preferred to keep them to himself… not like me, I promise them a load of tom to entertain rich businessmen, and then maybe hitch up with them later.'

George is lost for words.

'I mean, if you think of it,' he continues, blowing cigarette smoke into George's face. 'They are taken to a posh restaurant, given a great free lunch, and, then if they like the bloke, they can agree to be screwed... for a price, that is… it's all up to them. Nobody forces them.'

George is itching to knock the hell out of Derek but is aware of his superior size, and that he appears to be surrounded by many acquaintances. 'So…' clearing his throat, he asks, 'so, you say that Buster did some recruiting of these women, but preferred to… you know, serve himself first?' His voice is now so tight and strained that it barely overrides the volume of the music.

'For sure… he was sometimes successful, but Buster was… I must admit… a bit of a perv.'

'What do you mean?'

'He always overdid things. He didn't have trouble finding babes because he was such a handsome bugger, but he often went too far.'

He briefly pauses.

'He was adventurous with his prick and liked to try new ways of fucking them.'

George's imagination is aflame with sordid images of unconventional sex.

'One of his favourite questions was to ask the babe, 'Where do you want it, expecting them to answer, try my earhole for a change. But he knew precisely where he really wanted to go.'

George feels nauseous.

'The problem with Buster began when he was in the reformatory and got mixed up with guys who wanted kinky male sex... if you know what I mean.'

George's mind is ablaze with fury.

'Are you okay, Pete?'

George is trying hard to contain his rising anger and disgust.

'You're looking very *skeef,* my China.'

'Yeah, it's... er... the fucking heat,' and he takes the menu to fan himself.

Sitting back and enjoying the rest of his brandy and coke, Derek continues, 'So, it was left mainly to me to get them interested in our private business. But like any business, some you win, some you don't.'

Now that Derek is opening up, George doesn't want to discourage him, and sits back to listen.

'Buster screwed this one pretty chick, who was on my list... and a hot... a really hot favourite with businessmen. But he went too far with this number, and she died of an overdose. I got to hear of this later from one of my contacts. Shame! She made me big tom.'

George is so wrought with rage that he can hardly get the words out. 'And that woman... was she a...?' And casually flicking cigarette ash onto the floor he tries to control his shaking hand and quavering voice, 'You mean, was she a housewife?'

George feels a spasm in his right knee cap.

'Ja, her name was Susan. She lived on the beachfront. She was the perfect choice.' He leans back in the chair, and boastfully explains the approach. 'Just think of it, Pete, all I had to do was to tell the bird to be available from noon to 4 in the afternoon, and that she would enjoy an all-expenses-paid, hi-life thrilling adventure.'

Derek smiles as he reminisces on his conquests. 'Look, let's be frank, many of these birds enjoy poking, so, it's an absolute pleasure for them.'

George doesn't want to hear another word from his foul mouth. He is feeling sick to the core of his stomach. He glances at his watch. 'Look, I've got an early morning appointment.' He stands up.

'By the way,' says Derek, oozing with confidence and almost mockingly, 'I've thought about your offer.'

George pauses.

'It's not for me.'

George nods, silently approving. Derek quickly drains his glass, stands up and looks George in the eyes saying, 'Perhaps it's my turn to offer you some profitable business.' With a coarse laugh, he adds, 'not with women, but something else that may interest you as a bloke in the motor trade.' George looks suspiciously at Derek and moves towards the door.

'Come,' says Derek, 'I want to show you something.'

He leads George along the gloomy passageway to the custom's gate where Derek extends a greeting to the customs official who lets them through with a knowing smile. A large passenger liner lies berthed before them and several seamen are coming on and off the ship.

'Do you want to try some great single malt whisky at a fraction of the cost?'

George enjoys a good whisky, especially as a nightcap so, although uneasy about the invitation, agrees to go onboard with Derek, who is well known among several members of the crew.

'Good to see you, matey,' a tall English merchant seaman says as Derek and George pass him on the gangway. 'You know the way,' he smiles.

Derek heads towards the crews' quarters to meet another acquaintance that ushers them into a cabin where they are offered generous tots of Glenfiddich whisky.

'This is my special boardroom,' Derek asserts with overweening bravado, 'I have half a dozen floating boardrooms that come from all around the world, where I conduct some very serious business deals.'

George wonders why he is being told this.

'Listen here Pete… that is your name, right?'

George, who is beginning to feel increasingly uncomfortable, nods. Derek turns to the seaman in the room who hasn't taken his eyes off George. 'This is Simon. He's my whisky man, but he tells me that he spells it differently.'

'Yeah, I'm Simon Doyle, and as an Irishman, we don't throw valuable things away, so we have an 'e' in our spelling of whiskey.'

George gives a forced smile, not caring two hoots about its spelling. Derek pours him some whisky and both he and Simon stare at him as he takes a sip.

He feels the golden liquid sliding down his throat, and forces out, 'Great stuff!'

Derek nods in satisfaction, breaking the tension, 'Of course, it is only the best, that's the way I do business. Simon is my contact who gets me almost anything and everything I need from overseas. Not so, Si?'

Derek sits down next to Simon, who says with a supercilious grin, 'This matey gives me the best deals you can imagine… and I get him the best babes he can afford.' And putting his arm around Simon, he declares as if he were the Town Crier, 'Simon's cock gets a standing ovation from Singapore to Simons Town. And if you don't believe me, ask the ladies at Smuggies, they'll tell you.' He gives Simon a knowing smile. 'And, what's more, Simon and his mates can bring in genuine car spares at a fraction of the price… nothing too big like an engine block, but things like carburettors and most other smallish stuff that you may need for your motor car business.'

'Tell us what you want, and I'll do the rest,' Simon asserts.

'Pete owns a secondhand car lot, and would need spares… spares that he can get dirt cheap, not so Pete?'

Simon quickly follows up, 'We are back in Durban about once every six weeks… that's not too long to wait, I hope.'

George can't think offhand of any particular vehicle part that he is searching for but is open to opportunities.

'For British cars, we have a very good contact at Leyland. This guy can give us the best possible price.'

'How do you get the stuff through customs?' George asks tentatively, without expecting an honest answer.

'Leave that to me,' replies Derek, looking cockily self-assured. 'Anything the size of a suitcase is fine.'

The three of them continue drinking for about an hour when Derek is summoned to the adjoining cabin, where he receives a small package from another crew member. 'How much do I owe you?' asks Derek in a drawl.

'This stuff's popular, so it's getting harder to get.'

Derek pushes a wad of notes into the man's hand and after a quick visual count, he smiles approvingly. 'You really want to know what acid means?' smirks the dealer. 'It's short for a Long Shagging Doodle.' The dealer laughs uproariously and unfolds a small piece of paper from his trouser pocket. Looking at Derek, he says, 'This stuff gives me goose bumps and much, much more…' and he puts the paper to his tongue before waving Derek goodbye. 'See you on my next trip,' and continues laughing.

George is agitating to leave and when Derek returns, he says he has an early morning appointment, whereupon they make their way off the ship and back through the customs gate. Derek, who is on first name terms with the customs official, slips him a R10 note. They agree to meet again soon and shake on it, giving the impression that they are now committed partners in smuggling contraband. But Derek's expression is far from friendly, and George knows that he has a much more important score to settle with this man that goes beyond spare parts.

Chapter 12

MG Sports

In the gloomy, still hours of the night, George finds himself ensnared in a terrifying dream. He sees himself walking through a thick, dark canopied forest with no way out, and a cluster of tall deciduous trees and plants cursing and laughing scornfully at him while pushing him down deeper and deeper into a large wormhole that drops to the centre of the earth. Suddenly, the treetops turn into fat red-feathered mocking roosters, calling him a cuckold and crowing for all the world to hear, 'Your wife is everyman's plaything… cock-a-doodle-do.' A bubbling brook turns into a vile stinking stream of polluted filth that washes over him like a tsunami. He awakes with a fearful jolt and lies on his back looking up at a white, blank ceiling, feeling intense anger towards Susan for her betrayal and hatred of the man who enticed her into the escort business. He curls up into a fetal position and returns to a restless sleep, awakening with the radio alarm announcing snippets of the SABC morning news.

The Foreign Minister says the government is not unduly concerned about the decision of the United Nations General Assembly to call on countries to voluntarily boycott South Africa because of its apartheid policy, as this is unlikely to have any significant effect.

Furthermore, George believes he'll have no problems importing spares for his vehicles with the contacts he has made through his shipboard contacts. In his mind, it is business before politics, coupled with an opportunity to keep close tabs on Derek to learn the full story of his late wife's deceit and true cause of death. It is early December 1962, some three months since her passing.

George's emotional angst looms large in the weeks leading up to Christmas. It's the time of the year when he and Susan did special things together, like taking Candice to the paddling pool and walks along the promenade or a sunset leisure cruise on the bay. But this year, it all feels so empty and depressing. However, he goes out of his way to make it joyful for Candice, taking her to Payne Brothers Department Store for a magic sleigh ride into Toyland to meet Father Christmas, who gives her a large Lucky Dip box that seems to contain all her secret desires, until she opens it to find a selection of colourful plastic and cardboard trinkets of no real value. George also takes her to South Beach that is alive with entertaining activities for children. She particularly loves the Punch and Judy show and becomes a willing audience participant shouting out warnings and instructions to Mr. Punch, who totally ignores them.

Christmas day is spent with Bessie who prepares a delicious turkey and ham spread, with Winnie bringing the plum pudding and brandy sauce, heavily laced with Commando brandy to enliven their festive wits. Candice sits at the lunch table, her eyes barely visible above the tabletop, and wearing a paper crown to make her feel like a beautiful princess for the day. She is delighted to have received a colourful dolls' house with furniture and two pretty dolls to take up residence.

By New Year, George is further determined to uncover the life that Susan had led and to bring those responsible for her downfall to book. He returns to work on the 3rd, full of renewed energy and hope. Halfway through the month, a very attractive young woman enters his secondhand car lot wanting to test-drive a sports car. Her bright blue eyes fix admiringly on an MG TD Roadster sports in which she visualizes herself sitting behind the steering wheel with her long blonde hair and scarf blowing back in the wind, an image captured in an advertising poster that she once saw. George approaches her in an exaggerated suave and debonair manner. 'Morning Miss!'

She runs her slender fingers across the bonnet.

'This is the best sports car that Britain ever produced,' he says, with eyes firmly fixed on her fine figure.

She gives him a searching look, 'Are you the owner of place?'

He nods with a smile and notices that she appears to be putting on a front in giving the car's bodywork a loving stroke while looking agreeably at him.

'It's British, you say?'

'Yes, but sadly, this city is pulling down all things British.'

'What do you mean?'

'Well, the Union Jack was removed from the City Hall last year, so, I'm left wondering what's next? Perhaps the royal titles and badges worn by the army?'

'What a pity!'

'Are you British?'

'My parents are… sometimes more British than the British.'

'Well, now that we've become a republic you can't have the Union Jack flying anywhere in this country.'

She stretches out her hand to open the driver's door but is beaten to it by George, who ushers her into the driver's seat. The delicate touch of her soft skin gives him a momentary thrill that quickens the pace of his speech. 'It's a bargain at R175,' he gabbles.

She looks stunning behind the wheel.

'Although this two-seater beauty is ten years old, she glides like a bird.'

He waits for some response, thinking the price may remove the smile from her pretty face, but she keeps smiling, and asks, 'Can I take a test-drive?'

George pulls back the canvas roof cover and gets in beside her. 'This is the way to truly experience a great ride,' he oozes with a salesman's buttered tongue, loving the intimacy of her presence.

With the key already in the ignition, she starts the engine, its confident roar setting the tone for their test drive along the Snell Parade. The accelerator opens up its potential, and they drive onto the street with her long blonde hair sweeping back in the wind. Her smile broadens as she exclaims, 'This is the most exhilarating moment of my day.' Near the Natal Military Command, she stops, turns to George and says invitingly, 'I want it.'

He instantly dismisses what could be a double entendre and replies, 'Good, let's head back to the office and tie up the paperwork.'

'By the way, my name's Jane.'

'And I'm George.'

'I'm glad to meet the owner of George's Used Cars,' she says rather pointedly.

'Thank you, and I'm very glad to meet you.'

On the way back to the car lot, they stop at an intersection near Addington Hospital where Derek happens to pull up alongside. He leans across his passenger seat and shouts, 'Nice one there, Pete,' and roars off.

'Did that man just call you Pete?'

'I think he's confusing me with someone else.'

Derek slows down when he sees the MG turn into Point Road and tails them past George's Used Cars. George is unnerved by the experience, but he tries to stay cool in the presence of Jane.

Inside the office, he explains that he has to get the car licensed with a COR before she can take delivery in some three to four days.

'About payment... what is it to be? Hire purchase or...'

'Cash. I'll give you a bank guaranteed cheque.'

He smiles, as it doesn't come better than that! On taking down her details, George notices that she has a part-time job as a bookkeeper at an engineering firm, and lives in a flat along North Beach. He is dying to ask her on a date but considers the moment inopportune and decides to wait until the car is ready for delivery.

That Thursday evening, he is invited to supper at his mother's place along with Candice, who arrived earlier and is seated on the carpet playing with her dolls while Bessie is in the kitchen preparing the meal. She has prepared George's favourite dish, roast beef and baked potatoes to be followed by jelly and custard.

George breaks the news about Susan's financial state, 'A letter arrived for Susan in the post today.'

Bessie pauses to listen.

'Apparently, she had a savings account at the United Building Society. It's quite substantial.'

'How much?'

'Nearly R550.'

'Whew! Where did she get that from, I wonder?'

George is not prepared to disclose his suspicions, 'I have no idea… could be commission from her part-time marketing job.'

'Well, that can certainly help with expenses. Lucky boy!'

Their conversation is interrupted by a knock at the front door. Standing in the doorway and looking slightly ridiculous is Charlie holding a bunch of flowers and a bottle of wine. He brings his beloved Chooks into the hallway, leans it against the wall and kisses the handlebars before giving Bessie the wine and flowers. He and George sink into a conversation on the couch about the day's highlights when George mentions the pretty young woman, who had given him the best sale of the day.

'She's a stunner, Charlie! She's only been in Durbs for about two months, or, so she says, and from what I can gather, she doesn't have a boyfriend.'

'Get in there, young man. Don't miss out.'

'I plan to ask her out when she comes to fetch the car.'

'What did she buy?'

'An MG TD sports.'

Bessie enters the dining room carrying a tray of piping hot roast beef and roast potatoes. 'What's this I'm hearing about dating some pretty woman?'

'That's right, Ma, I can't stay single forever.'

'You shouldn't rush into these things. It's not right that you should want a relationship so soon after Susan's death.'

'I'm not marrying the woman. I'm just asking for a date.'
She gives George a strong disapproving look.
Bessie calls out, 'Candice, come, my darling, dinner.'
'First, go wash your hands,' adds George, trying to make a good impression as a caring father.
'You need a wife to handle all that stuff, George,' interjects Charlie while pouring the wine, and giving Bessie a generous helping.
'George doesn't need another woman in his life. He and I can handle the domestic things quite well together, not so George? So, stop interfering.'
Charlie is critical of Bessie's obsessively protective behaviour towards her son and hopes that she isn't going to be an obstacle in George finding a new female companion. After the main meal, Bessie offers dessert, but George declines saying he has business to attend to.
'But it's your favourite… jelly and custard.'
'Sorry, Ma, I must go.'
Bessie quickly checks Candice's homework, which consists of learning the words of the nursery rhyme, *'She'll be coming round the mountain when she comes…'*
"Check the origins of that one, Bess,' interjects Charlie, 'it comes from an old religious song about Jesus returning on the last day in a chariot.'
'Oh, stop talking nonsense and go home!'
Bessie kisses Candice goodnight.
'I'm not going anywhere until I have given you a sweet nightcap,' and he recharges Bessie's glass having waited anxiously for this moment to be alone with her to clear the air regarding his disastrous liaison with Winnie on the lounge couch.
'About the other day…'
Bessie is bending down to take a bowl of jelly from the fridge. 'I don't want to hear about it.'
'Why? I need to explain.'
'No need to explain anything, I was disgusted to the back teeth!'

'Okay, so, I've disappointed you.'

Bessie huffs and sighs.

'But listen, Bess, I've come to learn that it's silly to be disappointed in people… and that I've learnt from Mutt and Jeff.'

'Mutt and Jeff! What are you talking about, you idiot?'

She slaps down a bowl of jelly that wobbles in fury in front of him. 'My poor George, who loves his jelly, didn't have time for this because his head's full of another woman.'

'You know, Bess, my Mutt and Jeff…'

She gives him a threatening look, saying, 'Stop talking rubbish!'

'You know, the stray cats that hang around my flat at night. Well, sometimes I let the furry buggers inside, but then they disappoint me.'

Bessie is busy rolling up a newspaper.

'In the morning, Mutt leaves a big turd on the carpet… and Jeff… well, it's the bladder with him… he piddles all over my radiogram. He seems to time it with the SABC news bulletin when he turns my lounge into the Mangrove Swamp.'

Bessie gives him a fierce scowl, 'Come… I've heard enough of your filth!'

She tries to shoo him off the chair with the newspaper. When he doesn't move, she hits him over the head with it.

'Come on, get out of here you dirty beast. Can't eat with the likes of you. You belong in a pigsty.'

Shielding himself from the blows, Charlie replies, 'They only do it when my back is turned… and I don't want to say anything nasty about the newsreader, Paddy O'Byrne… because I think he's great, but they do it behind my back when I'm asleep. You must then reason… as with cats, so with pigs, dogs, sheep, lions, lizards, ants, tadpoles and turtles…' He continues to rattle off a long list of creatures while shielding her blows and taking rapid mincing steps towards the hallway where old Chooks is parked. Finally, he bravely turns around, 'And that's not excluding the Bessies, Winnies and Charlies… we all do it!'

'I do nothing of the sort! Now, get out!'

She gives him one hefty blow that sends him sprawling

CASTLES *in the sand* – *a riveting social drama*

backwards across the floor.

A knock at the front door brings an end to her tirade.

'Who on earth could that be?' she asks, quickly straightening her hair.

She opens the door to a postman holding a telegram. Her heart skips a beat thinking it conveys bad news.

'Please sign here, Mrs. Cooksley,' and he gives her the telegram.

'I get so darn nervous opening a telegram after dark. Thank you,' and closes the door.

From the floor, a guilt-stricken Charlie looks up at her.

Hesitant to open it, she says, 'It must be a mistake. It's not my birthday. But here it says... as clear as daylight, Mrs. Bessie Cooksley, Princes Street. I'm terrified to open it.' She offers it to Charlie. 'Here, you open it.'

'Maybe my brother in Cape Town has had a heart attack,' she mutters nervously. 'He drinks like a fish!'

Charlie tears open the envelope, takes one look at the message, and quickly hands it back to her. He then slowly creeps away to the kitchen to hide inside the broom closet from when he hears an outburst of expletives and curses.

'Just let me get my hands on that blighter! Charlie Blignaut! Now, where's that swine gone?'

Looking around the dining room she hears a noise from the broom closet.

'Hey, come out of there at once,' and she yanks open the door. 'What's the meaning of this?' holding up the telegram as if it were a piece of filth. 'Giving me such a terrible fright!'

She is interrupted by a knock at the front door.

'You sit down in that chair. Sit! I'm not finished with you yet.'

She struts with a determined marching step to the front door.

'Oh, God! It's you!'

'I'm so sorry I'm late, but my Reg... drunk again, he was. He started swearing at the neighbour. Yes, he told Mr. Venter to... he used a terrible f-word! Well, you can imagine, what Mr. Venter thought of that! He wanted to call the police.'

'My poor dear, sister, come on inside. I'm just trying to deal with a maniac.'

'Who?'

'Never mind.'

Winnie sees Charlie sitting like a naughty boy in the corner of the kitchen.

'There's plenty of food left, so don't worry. I'm just putting Charlie Blignaut in his place.'

Charlie gives Winnie a sheepish smile.

'I was just about to throw him out.'

Winnie sits down at the kitchen table and Charlie remains in the corner looking most forlorn.

'Hello, Charlie,' Winnie says with a sweet smile.

Charlie is about to reply but is cut short by Bessie. 'Don't speak to the brute. He's up to his old tricks again.'

'Why? What's he done?'

Bessie waves the telegram in front of Winnie. 'It's his idea of a joke.'

'What makes you think that, Bess?' But she doesn't reply.

With her curiosity aroused she asks Bessie, 'What does it say?'

'Ask Mr. Blignaut.'

'What did you say to Bessie?'

Feeling acutely embarrassed, he says to Bessie, 'Tear it up. Just tear it up.'

'So, I'm right then, this is just your idea of a joke.'

'It's not a joke, but if you think it is, then tear it up!'

'Is it something dirty, Bessie?'

Bessie goes right up to Charlie and stares him down.

'Why in a telegram? Why not come straight out with it?'

Charlie stands up, puts on his bicycle trouser clips and moves towards the kitchen door where he pauses. 'I just thought it would be a nice way to say it. That's all! So just forget it!'

As Bessie's anger abates, she begins to look at him somewhat piteously. 'Listen here, you bleery old fool, you're not proposing to *Tickey the Clown*. If you're asking me to marry you, then cut out all this hop, skip and jump nonsense with candles, home fires and telegrams… and just come to the point.'

'Marriage! Is that what he wants?' blurts out Winnie, feeling deeply hurt and rejected.

'Here, read it!'

Crestfallen, Charlie makes his way to the front door.

'Hey, Charlie Blignaut, just where do you think you're sneaking off to? Come back here and have some pudding. And stop trying to distract me with marriage proposals… old slab of misery! Come here.'

Glancing at Winnie to confirm that she, Bessie, has always been the favoured one, she gives Charlie an affectionate peck on the cheek.

'But listen here, Charlie boy, I can't be rushing off into marriage at my age. I've got a purpose here. My George needs me. It's not that I don't like you. No, you mustn't think that you silly old poep from the GPO,' and she gives him another quick peck on the cheek.

Winnie grimaces, *'I wish they wouldn't do that while I'm eating my food,'* she mutters to herself.

With the tension released, Charlie begins to assert himself, 'You need to start a new life, Bessie. You're making a big mistake staying here, that's all I say.'

'Hey, don't start lecturing me on things you know nothing about. Besides, George is now courting another woman, and that woman can never be a mother to his child.'

'Your son's a grown man. Let him get on with his life.'

'Just think for a minute, Charlie Blignaut, how can I marry you? Use your commonsense.'

'What's wrong with me? Am I not good enough?'

'I'm sorry, but I just can't see myself as Mrs. Charlie Blignaut.'

'What's so bad about that?' he asks in a dejected tone of voice.

'Ag, Charlie, don't make me say these things.'

'So, it's my name! You don't like my name, that's it, hey?'

'Ag, Charlieee!' she exclaims exasperatedly, elongating the last syllable in a shrill tone.

'That's okay, I understand. If you don't like my name, I'll change it.'

'You can't just change a name. It costs money.'

'This won't cost a cent because from now on you can call me Charles.' He braces himself smartly. 'How's that for a no-cost name change?'

'Ag, don't be stupid, man! You can't just be a Charles overnight. You've got to grow into your name.'

Charlie flops down dejectedly on the couch. 'Nothing I ever do pleases you, does it?'

She looks him up and down. 'For a start, you've got to look like a Charles. Those corduroy trousers and veldskoens will have to go. You'll have Winnie saying that I've come down in the world, not so Win?'

Winnie has removed herself from the conversation and unrolled the evening newspaper that was left lying on the floor to read the headlines.

'Not so Winnie?' Bessie repeats loudly.

Winnie looks up and raises her eyebrows in feigned disinterest.

'I'm comfortable in my clobber. Don't you agree Winnie?'

'Oh, yes, indeed you are,' she replies, suddenly coming alive and giving Charlie an endearing smile.

'Forget the comfort, think of the image,' insists Bessie. 'I can't be seen in public with a dopey hillbilly.'

Bessie walks slowly around Charlie as if examining a piece of merchandise. 'I want to take a good look at you, Mr. Charles Blignaut. For a start, I want a French pronunciation of your surname to sound like *Bleenou,* and not the Afrikaans, *Blig* with its guttural g that belongs in the gutter... making it sound like a swear word. What's more, I can't have a surname ending with the word, *no.* That's not good enough for me! Sorry!'

She keeps a sharp focus on him before demanding, 'Take off your *veldskoens.*'

'But Bess!'

'Don't but me, just take them off.'

Winnie drops the newspaper to stare at the goings-on.

'Now, the bracers!'
'My bracers! Never!'
'Don't argue!'
'What are you getting at? I don't understand. Why?'
'Stop whimpering like a booby and take them off.'
'No!'
'Charlie Bignaut, do I have to remind you what you promised? You said you'd do anything for me.'
'Did I?'
'Yes, now take them off.'
'Ja, but I meant within reason,' he squirms while releasing his bracers.
'Now, take those silly bicycle clips off your trousers.'
She pulls them off and tosses them aside.'
'Now, drop your trousers.'
'Never!'
'I'll give you a clip across the earhole if you don't do what I say.'
'You're going too far.'
'Stop acting like a stuck-up virgin, I know you better than that. Now, drop them.'
'No!'
'Yes.'
'No!'
She raises her right hand to clout him. 'Yes, yes, yes... I've seen it all before.'
Charlie drops his trousers to the floor.
'I'm sorry I gave you all that wine to drink,' he groans.
'That's a good boy! Now, you stay right there until I get back.' Noticing Winnie with her hand in front of her mouth giggling, she takes Charlie by the shoulders to turn him around. 'Winnie doesn't want to look at your banana hammock.'
Bessie gathers his discarded garments and goes through to the adjoining bedroom. Winnie is still giggling away while Charlie searches for something to cover himself, but the nearest thing to hand is the bunch of flowers left wilting on the sideboard. He

grabs them to dangle in front of his crotch while banging on the bedroom door. 'Bessie, come back with my trousers.'

'You can come and sit next to me, if you like,' coos Winnie with a smile, making room on the couch.

Charlie ignores the invitation and continues banging on the door.

'Bessie!'

'Stop shouting, man! You'll upset Candice next door.'

'I want my trousers.'

Bessie enters the lounge carrying a suit and a pair of slippers. 'Here, try this on. The man who wore these walked off this earth many moons ago. He was about your size. Pity about the shoes, but I gave them to the gardener, but here, try on his slippers. Take the flowers away from that thing of yours and hurry up and get dressed.'

Charlie obediently puts on the suit, which fits him rather well.

'I'll make a proper gentleman out of you yet, *Mr. Charles Bleenou!* You look quite handsome in a pinstriped suit. What do you think, Winnie?'

'I think you've made him look like a tropical fish.'

'What nonsense! You're just jealous.' Bessie gives him an admiring look. 'Come here, *Mr. Charles Bleenou, Esquire,*' and kisses him on the cheek. This is like an electrical current to Charlie, who demands to know where his trousers are, as he wishes to fetch something from the pocket.

'They're on the bed next door.' He quickly disappears into the bedroom and while he's out Bessie lights a candle and puts a Vera Lynn record on the turntable.

'I can be very romantic, when I choose,' she says on Charlie's return and gives Winnie, who is sitting in the glow of candlelight a cheeky glance, as if to say, he's mine whenever I want him.

Advancing on him with an exaggerated smile, Bessie coos, 'Shall we dance, *Monsieur Bleenou?*'

'Certainly, Madame Cooksley.'

They do a few turns on the floor when Charlie stops to take a little black jewellery box from his pocket and removes a silver diamond ring, which he tries to slip onto her engagement finger.

'What are you trying to do?'

'It's an engagement ring, Bess.'

There is a sudden change in Bessie's attitude as she realizes that her game has gone too far.

'Wow! Wow! Wow! Just hold on there a minute. You're rushing me! A ring! Now, that's different.'

'What do you mean, different?'

'You know what I mean, it's something that everyone sees.'

'Well, isn't that the point of getting engaged, so that everyone knows about it?'

'But you don't understand. If I wear a ring, it's for real. It's for… definite!'

'But that's the whole idea,' he says bitterly, putting the ring back in its box and placing it on the sideboard.

Bessie slinks into the couch next to Winnie. 'I thought we could just imagine it. Enjoy it as make-believe, so, when we go out to the movies, you can look smart and not like an overgrown Billy Bunter.'

'So, this was just a game?'

'Well, not quite a game… but… a way of knowing how it could turn out.'

'Okay, I get it. I get the whole picture now.'

Charlie returns to the bedroom to change back into his own clothes. Bessie re-organizes the lounge the way it was, switching on the light, blowing out the candle and taking the remains of the wine and glasses into the kitchen. Charlie emerges from the bedroom, pockets the ring he had left on the sideboard, puts on his bicycle clips and wheels old Chooks to the front entrance, pausing briefly to glance back at the two women sitting on the couch. Winnie's heart pines as she would dearly love to have been the woman he chose, while Bessie watches him go in silence, knowing that she has once again dominated the scene.

Chapter 13

A Date

George waits anxiously for the day when Jane fetches her MG, and when she phones on Monday morning to say that she'll be there by lunchtime his brain is awash with good-feel hormones, scheming how to arrange a date. He has all the relevant registration papers, log book and the receipt for the bank-guaranteed cheque enclosed in a smart-looking folder. He wants to make the transaction look seemingly casual as he intends to ask her to join him afterwards for a snack at the XL Tearoom on South Beach. Jane is dropped off in an Eagle Taxi and steps onto the showroom floor like a beautiful, sleek raptor ready to ensnare her prey. All male eyes rivet attention on her shapely legs and smooth, silky skin as she walks up to George, who promptly jumps to his feet to greet her. He eases the pace of his speech, to disguise his dopamine fueled enthusiasm.

'Hello, George… or, Pete,' she croons with a smile that almost wraps George's tongue up against his palate as he attempts to make a suitable reply. He stands and stares at this peroxided beauty as if she were the latest model on the showroom floor.

'Well, aren't you going to greet me?'

'Yes, yes, of course. By the way, forget about that other name! The guy doesn't know me from a bar of soap.'

'But I like the name, Pete.'

'Well, coming from your lips I have no objection.'

George begins to take control of his erratic breathing, saying, 'Here are all the papers. The car's officially yours.'

Jane sweeps across the showroom floor to put herself behind the steering wheel.

'Come, big boy! Let's take a ride,' she says in a whimsical tone of voice.

Thrusting the folder in front of her, he apologetically says, 'Wait, wait! You have all this to sign first.'

She struts back to his desk, briefly scans each page of the documents before putting her elegant signature to conclude the deal. Following the formalities, Jane is once again behind the steering wheel with George sitting like a well-groomed fox hound next to her. She takes off on the showroom's highly polished floor surface with all four wheels doing a sideways glide as if performing a French Chassé dance routine, before taking firm traction on the road outside.

'Where to?' she asks invitingly?

George racks his brain but before he can answer, she raises the stakes for something special. 'What about the Edward?'

George gets a sense that she's role playing but can't imagine why as she is so compellingly attractive, that she doesn't need to add airs and graces.

'Well, the Edward would certainly suit your glamorous image… but, if you want something that's a little more downbeat, there's the XL Tea Room right on the beach.'

'The XL! You're a cheapskate!'

Embarrassed that she should think that, he tries to recover his image by explaining, 'Just watching the budget.' He also thinks that having done a profitable sale, there's no purpose in going posh to impress her.

'I hope you're not a meanie.'

George swallows hard, not wanting to give the impression that he is not a man of means.

'Right!' he declares, with the enthusiasm of a tired ricksha puller. 'The Edward it is!'

They dine at the sumptuous smorgasbord restaurant, where

they add chilled white wine to a menu of specially chosen gastronomic delights. George throws all caution to the wind and is not concerned that the final bill will take a nibble out of his profits because to be seen with Jane has enhanced his self-esteem and brought back a load of fun and happiness into his life. Jane appears to be so self-assured and competent that she can steer any relationship in the direction she wants. She likes George, finding him physically attractive with a personality to match, not just for a one-off date, but one that could possibly sustain a deeper relationship. George succeeds in getting a yes for a night out at the movies. He cannot believe that they have clicked so easily and so soon. What strikes him about Jane is that she is so different to Susan, but he also senses that her outward show of confidence is masking something that she is suppressing.

After dating for about a fortnight, George is drawn increasingly to having an intimate relationship and invites her to take a stroll along the beachfront one evening. They find a spot on the soft, sandy beach where they sit and talk under a bright full moon reflecting off the surface of a calm sea.

'There's still so much about you that I don't know.'

Her blue eyes glitter in the light of the shimmering moon… she falls silent for a moment before turning to him, 'You told me about your ex-wife and that she died of an overdose.'

Reluctant to talk about Susan, George drops his head. 'I'm not entirely convinced of that… but her official death certificate records suicide.'

He lifts his eyes to look out upon the far distance of a shimmering, grey ocean, thinking that if he had to dive to its deepest depths to get to the truth about Susan's death, he would do so. He gently takes Jane's hand. 'Let's leave the subject for now.'

But Jane's curiosity has been aroused and she wants to know more. 'Was she beautiful?'

'Yes.'

She introspects for a moment. 'I grew up believing that when anyone said I was beautiful it would be when people wanted me to feel happy.'

George is confused.

'I was overweight as a child and still remember the day at school when boys crowded around me in the playground calling me a fat ugly cow.'

'They're stupid!'

'Maybe… but it had its upside because when I was in matric my father asked me to promise God that I would never have sex until I was married... and believing that I was an ugly cow made it easier to keep the wolves at bay. After all, if they were genuinely interested in me it would not be on account of my looks.'

George can't believe that she has such low self-esteem and can't stop admiring her lovely facial features and fair complexion reflected in the soft glow of the moonlight.

'In my teens, I found acceptance in a youth group of mainly Methodists and a few Anglicans who met once a week to pray the rosary.'

'What's that?'

'A bead prayer.'

'Never heard of it!'

'My father, a Baptist minister… a truly wonderful man, whom I greatly love and respect, was strongly against my saying this prayer because he said that we should rather pray directly to God.'

'But you nevertheless went ahead, even though it offended him.'

She gives a disarming smile, 'I'm not one to be easily deflected, but I found it difficult at first to get into this long prayer because of its repetition. Although Catholics pray this prayer, our youth group felt that it was a respectful way to draw closer to Mary's son.'

George feels uncomfortable, and declares, 'You're talking to a heathen who never prays.'

'Silly man, you are praying all the time in everything you do and say. It just depends on who your recipient is.'

George listens with a dose of scepticism.

'Do you believe in an invisible world?'

'If something is invisible how can it possibly exist... that's beyond me.'

'You have to draw aside the veil that separates the seen world from the unseen world. If you think that everything in our vast universe is just matter, then you're only seeing what your two eyes can tell you, and not the full picture.'

'Look I have a standard ABC view of life. Anything beyond my five sense remains a mystery.'

She laughs, 'I don't think we should go further on this as we may lose each other, and I wouldn't want that to happen.'

'I think I know where you're coming from... a dad who is a parson... a religious upbringing, but that wasn't for me.'

'It's strange... although we live in a material world, I seldom prayed for material things.'

'Really! I thought that's what most people prayed for... more money, good health...'

Looking reflectively out to sea, she says, 'I just wanted to find peace... peace within myself. That's what I earnestly prayed for.'

'Did you get it?'

'In a dream, I nearly got it... came close, but there was one missing piece of the puzzle...'

She pauses before continuing as she worries that she could be opening herself to ridicule. But George's sympathetic look encourages her to continue.

'I can only ascribe it to a gift wrapped in a Mexican tilma.'

'What on earth are you talking about?'

'A tilma is a cloak worn by Mexican peasants. One of the girls in our group told us the story of the appearance of the Virgin Mary to a peasant named Juan Diego. I'm not sure if the story is true, but apparently, the Virgin's image miraculously appeared on the Mexican's tilma together with some Castilian roses that don't grow in the area.'

'Sounds like an interesting bedtime story,' he smiles.

'Funny you should say that because that same night I had

this strange dream about a gift box of roses that arrived on my doorstep. And each rose I picked up had a name. There was tenderness, kindness, consideration, courage, fortitude, generosity, helpfulness… all these wonderful things. I felt elated, and frantically began searching for peace, but in my dream, I couldn't find it.'

Looking at her with tenderness, 'What about beauty and love? Were they among the roses?'

'No, I didn't see them either.'

George isn't sure how to respond other than to say, 'I hope this didn't upset you because there's no real substance to a dream, so, don't worry about it.'

'Perhaps my father was right, I should never have joined that group.'

Jane begins fidgeting and blurts out, 'I really don't like talking about these things.'

She stands up, dusts the sand off her dress and moves to the water's edge. George doesn't want to end the conversation and follows her. 'The sea has a way of tugging at our memories,' he says.

'Perhaps it's something to do with the tides, in which case many of my memories should just drift out to sea and be lost forever.'

'Tell me about your ex-husband? Did he respect your wishes?'

'My wishes? What do you mean?'

'Well, about waiting until you got married.'

'My father made it clear to Johnny that his daughter was a virgin and would remain so until she married.'

George shakes his head in disbelief, and glad to have been spared such an injunction from Susan's father.

'It wasn't easy. But if men thought I was just an ugly cow I could at least offer them something pure and special on my wedding night.'

He turns to face her directly.

'Jane, listen… what if I tell you truthfully and sincerely that in your face… I see beauty. Would you refuse to believe me?'

She gives him a quixotic smile, suited to his chivalrous gesture, and looks away.

'Jane, look at me… you are beautiful. And you don't need a rose to tell you that.'

George gathers a handful of beach sand and holds it up to the light of the moon. 'I swear to the goddess of the moon, if there is such a creature, that you are a beautiful woman.'

She laughs, and says playfully, 'My noble knight in shining armour you are blind to the truth that lies within, only I can see that.'

'Take it or leave it, but that's my honest assessment of what I can see. Anything unseen I must leave to you.'

'Catch me!' And with splashing feet she runs along the water's edge with George running ahead, then turning around forcing her to run into his arms. She bursts out laughing. 'I'm not some mermaid to be tangled up in your arms.'

They move up the beach to find a dry spot to sit on. 'You know, the night that Johnny asked me to marry him, I thought he was making a big mistake. He must be crazy, I thought, wanting to marry me… because I couldn't see any man wanting to live with me for the rest of their lives'

'You're a crazy woman! So, what happened to break up the marriage?'

She pauses briefly looking at the retreating waves, 'Death! He was killed in a car crash.'

'I'm sorry to hear that.'

He expects a look of sympathy but is surprised to see her face set in a cold, steely expression. She lights a cigarette and looks out upon a deep and restless ocean.

George finds her so opposite to the extravert he first met on the showroom floor, yet he is enchanted and drawn to her irresistible personality. They stroll back to her car parked on the beachfront. She doesn't resist a goodnight kiss.

Chapter 14

A Date with Death

It is 18 January 1963, and parliament in Cape Town opens with the United Party opposition leader, Sir De Villiers Graaff, spearheading his party's no-confidence debate. Although George is not involved in any political party, he admires De Villiers Graaff as a World War II veteran of integrity, who is more moderate in his racial views than the extremist stance adopted by Verwoerd's nationalist government. George listens with half an ear to the news knowing that De Villiers Graaff has no chance of bringing the National Party government down in a no-confidence debate. De Villiers Graaff has led his party into two successive defeats at the polls, and the party now finds itself fighting on two fronts since twelve of its former members left the party in 1959 to form the Progressive Party, although only one of them, namely, Helen Suzman, remains in parliament.

It's also on this day that George receives a message at work from Derek, who claims to have a new clutch plate kit for an Austin 1100, saying the price is well below retail, and that it comes off a ship directly from the factory in England. George thinks that it's a bit odd because the Austin 1100 was only coming onto the market in August that year, so why would they be making spares available now? But George is not one for turning down a bargain, knowing that an 1100 could well be on his showroom floor within the coming months. He looks again at the note, 'Meet me in Theatre Lane – just off West Street – at ten o'clock tonight. Bring at least R40.' He can't believe how cheap the offer is.

After making arrangements with his mother to have Candice sleep overnight at her house, he heads for the West Street Cemetery and arrives at the main gate in Theatre Lane at a few minutes to ten. As he waits, he becomes increasingly suspicious of Derek's intentions, but if he can get spares at such a low price it is worth the risk. Also, Derek is not as tough as his late brother and is therefore not a physical threat.

From his rear-view mirror, he sees a black car pulling up behind him with two occupants in the front. Derek gets out of the driver's seat and approaches George's vehicle. George leans across the front seat to open the passenger door. Derek gets in empty-handed.

'Where's the stuff?'

'In the boot of my car.'

'Who's the other guy?'

'He's off the ship and wants the money first. R20 for the carburettor.'

'But I thought you said you had a clutch kit?'

'Yeah, that too, but not tonight. Tonight, he's got a real bargain for you, twenty bucks for a carburettor.'

George hands him the cash.

'He's got other stuff he wants to show you.'

'What sort of stuff?'

In an ominous tone, Derek smirks, 'Come... come and have a look,'

He then flicks open a stiletto knife, and as George steps out the car he jabs the sharp point against the small of his back. Move you fucking bastard.'

George freezes in his tracks.

'What are you talking about?'

'Don't act the bloody innocent. Bastard! Peter Fucker!' He stares him down. 'I know who you really are.'

George is shaken by the accusation. Looking menacingly, Derek grinds the words between his teeth. 'You're fucking

George Cooksley… yes, you bloody liar. You killed my brother!'

George's mind goes into panic mode.

Derek, who had passed this way earlier in the evening to cut the gate chain to the cemetery, pushes open the wooden gate with his foot and shoves George through the entrance. His companion, a tall, burly man with a dark complexion and carrying a deadly hunter's knife, gets out the car and approaches George, whose mind is now flashing flight mode, knowing that if he doesn't do something immediately, he is dead meat. Derek grabs hold of his arm, but he breaks free and runs through a row of white tombstones dating back to the early settler history of the city. Derek shouts to his companion to cut him off to the right, while he makes for the cemetery chapel where George manages to outrun him and hides in a small alcove that Derek doesn't notice and runs past him towards the outer railing of the cemetery. This gives George time to head for the perimeter wall adjoining the Emmanuel Cathedral, where he scrambles over the brick wall and hides among the thick shrubbery. But when he hears Derek and his partner approaching and shouting his name, he flees across to the thoroughfare between the Parish Centre and the Cathedral where he finds a side door to the cathedral unlocked. He quickly ducks inside, shutting the door firmly behind him. The interior is dark and lit only by a small red lamp glowing near the altar. He slowly makes his way up the centre aisle to sit on the top altar step below the sanctuary light, his heart thumping furiously. Within the thick walls of the Cathedral, he can't hear any voices or noise from outside and is soon lulled into its solitude and silence. He checks the right side of the small of his back, feeling for any bleeding that Derek's blade may have caused. He wipes away a few drops of blood.

As a total stranger to this place of worship, his eyes sweep curiously across shadowy statues and huge crucifix, which all make little sense to him. Believing that his life is threatened should he step outside, he decides to spend the night within its safe confines, and is soon nodding off to sleep, only to be shaken awake at sunrise by a priest who enters the sanctuary to prepare for early morning Mass. George is at a loss to explain his presence, but ends up saying, 'I was chased by a gang of thugs through the cemetery and found safety here.'

The priest looks suspiciously at him, thinking that he, too, could be mixed up in some criminal activity.

'Well, you can't sleep here, young man. We have morning Mass in half an hour.'

George has no idea what Mass means but assumes it is some sort of religious service. He apologies for his intrusion and bids the priest goodbye. On the way out, he turns to say, 'I can't believe how peaceful this place is.'

'Come back anytime. You were sheltering under the tabernacle where the true presence of Jesus Christ resides.'

George ponders what he means, believing that Catholics indulge in some strange superstitious practices. He pauses, 'Thank you.'

'Come to Mass, it's a foretaste of heaven on earth.'

George makes his way along the pavement to where his car was parked in Theatre Lane, but it is gone. He takes a bus to the Point and arrives at work hungry and fearful, with the office telephone ringing incessantly. A recognizable angry voice curses him. 'Bastard! I'll get you yet!' and hangs up.

Shortly afterwards, his mother phones to ask why his car is parked in front of his home? George wastes no time and makes his way to the nearest gunsmith to buy a 9mm pistol, which he now carries on him for self-defence.

Chapter 15

Finding Love

In his early morning jog along the North Beach shoreline, George manoeuvres his way through a group of bathers and surfers silhouetted in the pallid mist, his mind all the while preoccupied with chartering a safe passage through a haze of intrigue and tension that has beset his life. He is in a quandary about his encounter with Derek. If he takes the matter up with the police it will be his word against Derek's, and the fact that a charge of culpable homicide was recently dropped against him, may tarnish his reputation in the eyes of the law even further. Moreover, the police are not going to offer him round-the-clock protection, so he is left to look after himself.

Meanwhile, George has taken over full ownership of the business, having paid out the final instalment to the previous owner who has retired. But he gets an unexpected visit from Basil Edwards, his former boss, who arrives on the premises with his lawyer, David Engelbrecht. George is reminded of the contract he signed on joining Edwards' firm, that prevents him from trading in the same or similar business for two years after leaving the company. Edwards pompously slaps the contract down on George's desk.

'You are in breach of this legally binding agreement.'

George briefly scans the document and remembers signing it without having given much thought to its consequences.

'We can take it to court if you like,' says his former boss.

George's business is doing well, and he is reluctant to give it up.

'Look, I'll need to show this to my lawyer.'

'There's not much he can do about it. It's a legally binding contract.'

'So, what do you want me to do? I'm not just getting up and walking away from this business that I have built up.'

'You could sell it.'

'That isn't going to help you. You'll still have competition, except it won't be from me.'

'I want to buy your business.'

'Oh, so that's what this is all about.'

George looks hard at his former boss, whose bushy eyebrows bristle in the sunlight streaming through an open window. George thinks this may be a way out of a dangerous area where Derek has much influence.

'Well, make me an offer, and I'll think about it.'

Although George has never liked Basil Edwards because of his irritating personality, he has to admit that he always conducted a fairly honest business.

'I know what other similar businesses in the area are going for, so, leave it with me for a few days, and I'll get back to you.'

'I'll give you seven days,' says Edwards.

The lawyer leaves a copy of the contract on the desk before departing.

In the meantime, George arranges to meet Jane for dinner that evening at the Beach Hotel. She parks her MG in front of the hotel, attracting admiring eyes that follow her lithe body into the foyer where George is anxiously waiting. An immediate magnetism brings him to his feet as he proudly escorts her into the dining room. She informs him that she has to vacate her accommodation as the owner has sold the flat.

'I have an extra bedroom,' he cheerfully offers.

Her immediate response appears negative.

'What about your daughter?'

'Candice would love to have a mom in the house.'
'A mom!'
'Candice misses a mother figure in the house.'
'If I agreed, it would only be for a short while, possibly a month or so, until I can find something else.'

George's eyes light up with a *'please, say yes'* expression. He waits patiently for an answer.

Almost teasingly, she says, 'We'll see.'

Several days later, George receives a phone call from her to say that she'd like to move in but insists on separate bedrooms. George is delighted with the news, but Bessie doesn't share his enthusiasm. She warns him against taking a strange woman into his house, and that it could upset Candice, as well as lead to scandal. George is not swayed, and on Saturday morning, Jane arrives and moves into the spare room with two large suitcases and a few small items of furniture. Candice, who is by nature shy and reserved, politely smiles when introduced but doesn't express any discernible emotions. Jane goes out of her way to make friends and suggests a trip to the beach the following morning.

George is finding it hard to check his emotions that are beginning to cloud his better judgment, and although he is not prepared to declare his feelings for her at this stage, his actions are those of a man who is smitten. He is almost craven in the way that he wants to ensure that her stay will be pleasant, insisting that he will do anything to make her happy. Despite his mother's negative comments, he believes that once she gets to know Jane and her Baptist background, she will have a changed attitude. No invitation for dinner is received from Bessie, so George decides to rely on the traditional Thursday evening arrangement when he, Susan and Candice would often have dinner with her. He phones his mother on Thursday morning saying that the three of them will be coming around for dinner that evening. He barely waits for a reply before adding, 'I have to rush. See you at 6.30.'

When they arrive, he is expecting a cold reception, but Bessie warmly welcomes Jane into her house. She has laid out her finest porcelain crockery and Sheffield silver cutlery. Winnie is also present, acting as a waitress in serving pre-dinner drinks and snacks. Later she helps her sister in laying out the food on the table. George not only sighs with relief at what he sees, believing that this augurs well for his future relationship with Jane. Bessie had spent time that afternoon putting her hair in large curlers to create a bouffant, adding to an overdone appearance.

On sitting down to eat, Bessie goes out of her way to engage Jane in conversation and asks about her family, and, in particular her Baptist minister father. Bessie has no allegiance to any religious denomination, although acknowledges a belief in God, but one that is moulded to fit her personal view of the world.

Not being sensitively selective in her subject, Bessie declares, 'I think there is far too much talk about hell and punishment in the Bible.'

'Good and evil have their place,' replies Jane, not wanting to engage in a religious argument.

Bessie enquires with a smile, 'What was it like being brought up by a church minister?' expecting to hear about a very restrictive childhood but is disappointed to hear Jane's reply. 'I had a beautiful childhood... a very happy one. My father was loving and kind.'

'Oh, so you've had a very happy life?' she enquires with a tinge of disappointment in her voice.

'My troubles are largely the result of my own making.'

Bessie waits to hear more, but Jane is not forthcoming until asked a direct question. 'So, I gather you were married...'

Jane pauses, glances at George and then gives a curt reply. 'I had a very unhappy marriage... but I'd rather not go into details.'

George decides it's time to change the subject and turns to Winnie. 'My aunt was once a full-time nurse at Addington, but now works there on a more flexible basis.'

Winnie, who loves to shine in the company of visitors, says with exaggeration, 'Caring for other people gives me a great sense of satisfaction... and, even if I may say so, a sense of joy.'

Bessie frowns with disdain, knowing that Winnie is often as

lazy as an old sow, but grudgingly gives her a dash of credit, 'Yes, my sister enjoys being a slave as you may have noticed, always wanting to put herself upfront in whatever she does.'

Winnie is used to her sister putting her down and continues smiling graciously, saying, 'My sister always knows everything about everybody, even when she doesn't know anything at all.'

Bessie bites her lip and gives Winnie a spiky-eyed look before turning with a syrupy smile to Jane, who is about to tuck into the main course. 'How do you like the roast beef? It's George's favourite. Only I know how to make it special for him.'

George cringes with embarrassment.

'Oh, it's lovely, thank you. Quite delicious!' replies Jane, thinking that George's mother has an unhealthy fixation.

Candice quietly eats her dinner while soaking up everything she hears and sees, believing that Jane is a nice lady that she can get to like very much. George cannot believe how pleasant the evening has been, thinking his mother has at long last accepted a woman that he loves. Even Winnie is surprised by her sister's welcoming attitude, but that all changes when she and Bessie walk George, Jane, and Candice to the front door to say goodnight. The door is no sooner closed than Bessie turns to Winnie.

'The bitch! I can see right through her!'

Chapter 16

Fresh Proposals

George's business is not far from Smuggies and the location where Fort Victoria had once stood as a bulwark against attacks from the Zulus. But that was back in 1838 when a detachment of the Seaforth Highlanders was sent to protect the Port Natal settlement, whereas today George seeks protection from a white thug who has already tried once to kill him and continues to threaten his life. Since the encounter in the cemetery, he has been constantly on the alert, expecting a return visit from his nemesis at any moment.

The following morning, he receives a menacing telephone call but it's not from the person he anticipates.

'Well, Cooksley, have you made up your mind?' It is David Engelbrecht, the lawyer, who has now adopted an aggressive manner.

'If your client meets my price, we have a deal.'

'What is your price?'

'My stock is my main asset, so you'll need to come over and we can work something out.'

'Yeah, but I'm not taking your valuation. I'll bring an expert with me.'

'Save yourself the time and money, I've got the Auto Dealer's Guide which is used by everyone in the trade... even insurance companies have copies.'

'Are you available at midday?'

'Yup! Be my guest.'

George gives thought to what he will do once his business is sold. He wants to get away from the Point area, as there are too many memories of Susan and the sinister presence of Derek.

When Engelbrecht arrives, he and George spend the next four hours calculating the value of his company's assets. They take into account the stock as well as additional values, such as location and goodwill, arriving at a figure of R65,000, but after subtracting the company's liabilities they are left with a total of R32,000. The lawyer takes the offer away to discuss it with Edwards.

George can't wait to get home that evening to discuss the future with Jane and Candice.

'I think we can be out of here in about two months, three at the most. I'm going to look to opening a small business either in town or in the Umbilo area.

Jane appears delighted but still insists that she will be out of George's home within a month. This brings George to the realization that he wants Jane to be part of his life, not simply as a border biding her time, but in a long-term relationship. He invites her out the following evening to have dinner at Claridges Hotel on the beachfront, preceded by drinks at Cookie Look, the hotel's first floor bar and dance venue.

Before ordering drinks, Jane goes to the Ladies toilet, and on her return pauses briefly at a table to exchange words with a man sitting next to a woman and out of sight of George. Meanwhile, George's mind is in a whirl as he prepares to navigate a conversation that steers clear of Jane's beauty, but one that cannot disguise his growing affection for her. On returning to her seat, Jane looks slightly unnerved.

'You know, I've been thinking that if I can establish a new business, there's no reason why you can't be a part of it.'

Jane doesn't appear to hear him.

'Hey, Jane! Did you hear what I said?'

Snapping out of it, she replies distractedly, 'Sorry, George, I had something on my mind.'

'I was saying that I'd like you to be part of my new business.'

Looking embarrassed. 'Yes, yes... thank you. It's something to consider.'

'Are you sure you're feeling okay?'

'Absolutely, I just felt a little queasy. I think it was something I had eaten earlier.'

Trying to brighten up the conversation, he says, 'Did you know that two years ago, Cliff Richard and the Shadows stayed in this very hotel?'

'No, I didn't know that. I love their music.'

'Me too.'

He sees her face beginning to lighten up.

'They were on a concert tour of South Africa.'

With the conversation taking a light and engaging tone, George is unaware of his nemesis sitting next to a brassy woman in the far corner of the room. But shortly afterwards, when Derek walks out with the woman, George catches sight of him and his face contorts with intense anger, knowing that at some stage soon he is going to have a head-on clash with the man. Jane, aware of his sudden unease, tries to deflect the conversation by referring to his conflict with Edwards and the sale of his business, saying, 'I understand, it must be tough for you to let go of a successful business.'

George picks up on her cue. 'I was thinking about what the lawyer said, that my business would never prosper in that particular location, which is a lie.'

'Don't upset yourself. You have been made a good offer. Wait and see what happens.'

At the dinner table, George is more relaxed, and his focus is entirely on the woman he has fallen in love with. During their dessert, he musters the courage to ask if she would marry him. Jane is taken aback and initially left speechless.

'I hardly know you, George...'

'I know, but I am being honest with my feelings for you.'

Jane's mind is filled with self-doubt and confusion.

'No-one should rush into a marriage just on feelings.'

He leans back and smiles. 'Why do you always have to be so correct about everything?'

'It's just the way I am.'

'Would you consider a period of engagement?'

She looks sympathetically into his deep-set eyes.

'I love you, Jane. And, that's more than just feelings talking.'

She looks down at her wine glass. 'I need time to think this through.'

He is reluctant to ask how she feels towards him, but at the end of the dinner, she says, 'You are one of the nicest men I have ever met.' But quickly looking away, she uses her failed marriage to turn down George's proposal which she knows inwardly she is not in a position to accept. 'My husband was very controlling. He was always criticizing me, putting me down in front of others, complaining about my appearance, calling me fat and saying he was embarrassed to be seen in public with me. As someone who came into the marriage with low self-esteem, I accepted what he said about me and when the physical abuse started, I almost believed that I deserved it. Then fate stepped-in when he was killed in a motor car accident.'

George listens with interest. She is speaking with confidence without the diffidence of before. She lights up another cigarette and continues. 'It is something I never want to live through again... so forgive me if I am somewhat reticent about jumping into another marriage, particularly to someone, who, although I feel drawn to, I barely know.'

George feels crushed.

Jane continues, 'After his death, I was determined to change my image, lose weight, dye my hair, buy fashionable clothes... and I joined an organization that helped abused women.'

George is at a loss for words. He reaches out to take her hand. 'What you have just shared reaffirms my feelings for you. What I'm looking for is a lifelong partner and friend... not a sexually alluring woman. Susan was a stunner, a head-turner you could say, but as much as I loved her, I never sensed that we had a really deep relationship.' He briefly pauses, and gazing longingly into her eyes, adds, 'which I now feel towards you.'

Jane is visibly moved thinking that perhaps, at last, she has found someone with whom she can form a meaningful relationship.

After dinner, they take a stroll along South Beach towards Addington Hospital and sit on the cool beach sand, enjoying the gentle crashing sound of the surf breaking along the shoreline. The fresh sea breeze coming off the Indian Ocean is like a sweet blessing from the unseen world that Susan so fervently believes in. They walk back to the maisonette in relative silence, locked in their private thoughts. George is dearly hoping that she'll say yes, while Jane remains in a state of doubt and confusion about her immediate future.

Bessie soon gets to hear about their dating and is very upset that George is planning to move out of the maisonette. She tries to dissuade him, and with moist eyes pleads for him to stay.

'You can't just abandon me, George. It's not right. You're my only child.'

'You've got Winnie to be on hand should you need anything important, like medical help…' he replies, trying hard to allay her fears.

'It's not the same. I sometimes need a man to… to fix things… and just to be around. I need you, my son.'

'You've got Charlie.'

'Heavens forbid! Don't ever leave me with that man alone.'

'I need to give Candice a home with a garden, close to a good school where she can make lots of friends… somewhere safe where she can have a normal childhood.'

'This is a wonderful area for any child to grow up. You have amenities here that you don't get anywhere else in the city. And it's no less safe than the suburbs.'

George discerns a growing tension and decides to cancel the regular Thursday evening visit, which makes Bessie even more resentful. She tells Winnie that she doesn't like the direction that the relationship is taking, and that Jane is proving to be worse than Susan.

George receives a call from Engelbrecht on Friday morning to say that his client is prepared to pay him R29,000 for his business. George is now eager to sell and makes a counter-offer. 'My bottom line is R30,000.'

'I'll get back to you.'

With the weekend ahead, George takes Jane and Candice up the coast to spend Saturday night at the Salt Rock Hotel. In walking with them along the beach the following morning, he points out the rugged rocks in the low-lying tide, saying, 'Zulu handmaidens collected salt off those rocks for King Shaka.' And clutching Jane's hand, adds, 'I think it has special properties that we should explore.'

He stands among the rocks scraping off tiny pieces of salt.

'Taste it.'

'Let me taste it, too, daddy.'

They all taste the salt.

George says with a beaming smile, 'I believe we've all been touched by the magic salt that flavours a romantic heart.'

'What does that mean, daddy?'

'That you, Jane and I now possess loving hearts… forever.'

Jane smiles and kisses George on the cheek.

'I also want to kiss my daddy.'

George lifts Candice into his strong arms. She embraces him around the neck, and with a smacking kiss declares in dulcet tones, 'I love you, daddy.'

Under a diaphanous blue sky Jane looks on with eyes bright with sunlight and happiness, but she keeps what she really feels locked deep inside.

Chapter 17

Decisions

Jane brings a fresh and joyful ambience to the home and together with her large collection of Long-Playing records has created a place of music and singing. Candice loves the songs of Eve Boswell whose *Sugar Bush* has her singing along with the Hungarian-born vocalist but finds her limited vocal range strained on some of the lower-pitched notes and quickly covers her mistakes with an engaging, apologetic smile. George goes out of his way to make Jane feel comfortable in his home, often bringing her flowers and chocolates, but behind this façade his mind is in turmoil regarding his feelings for her, his future business and the rift he would cause with his mother should he move away from Prince Street. He takes the first opportunity to speak with Jane about some of these pressing issues.

'When I spoke about a move to the suburbs... I think we should delay it by six months.'

'Please don't let me be a factor in your decision. I hope to be out of here within a few weeks.'

Shifting uncomfortably in his chair, he replies 'It's my mother, who is trying to persuade me to stay on.'

Disguising her true feelings, she says somewhat flippantly, 'She's a lovely person, although a feisty number at times, but... no need to hurt her feelings by leaving. So, stay on, for her sake.'

George is reminded of his conversation with Susan about

the same issue. Susan was anxious to move away, and he had promised to do so within a year. As an only child, he has a strong bond with his mother, but at the same time, he cannot suppress his deep feelings for Jane. He looks at her, hoping that she would reconsider his offer of marriage.

With Frank Sinatra singing in the background, *The Nearness of You*, he says to her, 'This is for you.' Her beautiful eyes brighten as the words of the song fill the room.

> *It's not the pale moon the excites me*
> *That thrills and delights me, oh, no*
> *It's just the nearness of you.*

George silently mouths the last line leaving Jane feeling very uncomfortable. She gets up and moves a few paces away, 'I can't understand why anyone would want to say that to me. I'm not that worthy.'

'Why do you have such a low opinion of yourself?'

She shakes her head and looks down.

George remains silent while the closing words of the song play out.

> *When you're in my arms and I feel you so close to me*
> *All my wildest dreams come true.*

Jane's mood changes and she says flippantly, 'You're quite a sentimental fellow,' and gets up to pour herself a glass of wine. The distance she is putting between them is hurtful to George, who replies in a matter-of-fact tone, 'Anyway, I'd like to hear the answer to my other proposal.'

She looks quizzical.

'About the sale of my business?'

'Oh, that!' she sighs with relief. She sits down next to him, her fragrant presence almost intoxicating him. 'Do you think Edwards will accept it?'

George looks appealingly at her. 'I'm fairly positive... as I hope to be with all my offers.'

She stubs out her cigarette, gets up and puts on the Beach Boys singing, *Surfin' USA*. 'Come, dance with me big boy.' They do a few quick turns around the room before ending up laughing and falling onto the couch. But before George can seize the opportunity for making love, she gets up declaring that she has a dental appointment.

The following day, George receives a telephone call from Engelbrecht.

'Mr. Cooksley, good morning.'

'Morning! I hope it's a good one.'

'Yes, indeed! Mr. Edwards has accepted your counter-offer.'

'Excellent!'

'It will be paid in three tranches. A letter will follow to give further details.'

'When does he want me out?'

'Is the end of the month too soon?'

'If he pays the first tranche by Friday, I'll make every effort to be out by the 30th.'

George is delighted with the news and his mind immediately goes into visualizing what he will do with the money. He phones Jane and arranges to meet her for lunch.

When they sit down at the table, George produces a small hand mirror to reflect the image of her face. 'I want to show you this... study it closely. It is the image of a beautiful woman... a woman that I love and hope to marry.'

She pushes the mirror away. 'Don't be silly, George.'

The restaurant ambience with its soft instrumental music in the background sets a romantic mood that unfortunately only George finds infectious. Not wanting to hurt him any further, Jane asks, 'George, do you think there is a difference between being in love... or simply loving someone?'

He looks confused.

'What if I told you that I love you, but wasn't sure at this stage whether I was in love with you?'

'How am I supposed to answer that?'

'I don't think you can. Only I can.'

'So, is that where we stand? You are not in love with me, but...?'

'Oh, George, just give me time. I have hang-ups that are getting in the way of our relationship. Let me deal with them in my own way.'

She gives him such an endearing smile that he has no alternative but to say, 'I leave it all to you,' then sits back folding his arms. 'I'm a patient man.'

George returns to work and sets about thinking seriously about his business future. He is not keen at this stage to start up another used car business, but as a technical boffin he looks at opportunities at several local engineering companies. He reads up about a company that manufactures automotive components and gives them a call. He is told to submit a job application.

While standing outside on the pavement of his car lot, Charlie happens to pass by on old Chooks, giving his buddy-bike a pat on the handlebars as he dismounts. He greets George warmly.

'Nice to see you, George.'

'Yeah, it's been some weeks since we last met.'

'Well, your Ma chased me out of the house, and I haven't been back since.'

'You must know her by this stage. Her moods change with the weather.'

'I'd appreciate it if you could put in a good word for me.'

'Sure, pal, I'll do that little thing for you.'

George updates him on what has happened in the interim since they last met, and how he has found the love of his life in Jane.

'Steady on there, George! These are matters of the heart and are not to be rushed.'

'Sure, but the heart beats impatiently.'

Charlie pedals on furiously down the road wearing a postman's cap, khaki shorts and a pair of old velskoens, hardly the image to arouse romantic yearnings in any woman, least of all in Bessie.

As George and Jane weren't invited to supper with Bessie

the previous Thursday and that he wanted to break the regular date, he is surprised to receive a call from her inviting him and Candice to come around. With awkward hesitation, he replies, 'Yes, but what about Jane?'

'Yes, yes, of course, George, you must bring her too.' And then as if she didn't know, asks, 'Is she still with you?'

'Yes.'

George detects a sudden change of tone in her voice but feels that his mother has no alternative but eventually to accept her.

'No, that's fine, my son! See you at 6.30.'

George worries that his mother is developing the same insane jealousy that she had towards Susan and decides to soften the event by taking her a bunch of flowers. When Bessie opens the door, she receives the flowers like a woman being courted and kisses George on the cheek. Her cheerfulness, however, cools on greeting Jane.

'Come inside... all of you. And here's my precious Candice,' and gives her a tight hug. 'How are you, my sweetheart?'

'Fine,' and she gives her granny a kiss.

None of the fine table linen or Sheffield cutlery is on display, but only a plastic tablecloth from the OK Bazaars is laid out with nondescript white crockery. Winnie hasn't been invited.

'Come, sit everyone.'

Jane hesitates a moment before taking the chair that George points out.

'We shan't be having pre-dinner drinks as I forgot to order a new bottle of sherry,' which is a lie as George notices a bottle tucked away at the back of the sideboard.

'So, how was your day, my son?'

'Getting things ready for the new boss. By the way, Charlie popped in to say hello.'

'I never want to see that scoundrel again.' She looks across to Jane. 'You have no idea what a nuisance he is. Comes around any time of the day or night with stories that no decent woman wants to hear. I told him not to come back again, as he wastes my time with his piffle.'

'As I was about to say,' interjects George, 'Basil Edwards takes over on the 1st of the month.'

'I never liked that Edwards fellow. You did the wise thing, my son, but I'm sorry you had to sell to that swine.'

'If I didn't, we would've ended up in court. He had a legal edge over me with his restraint of trade contract.'

'Anyway, never mind, you will surely get something going soon.' Turning to Jane, she says, 'My George is very clever with his hands. He matriculated at the George Campbell Technical High School and got excellent grades for his technical drawings.'

Jane smiles admiringly at George. 'I like a practical man, who can do things around the house, and also make a living doing what he enjoys.'

'Yes, yes, there's plenty of work George can do around my house, as I have kitchen cupboards that need fixing.'

'Don't worry Ma, I'll get around to doing it.'

'When?'

'Perhaps over the weekend.'

'Oh!' interjects Jane. 'I thought we were going to go to Margate this weekend as we had such a lovely weekend at Salt Rock.'

Bessie's eyes screw up in jealousy as she hears this and embarrasses everyone with an unwarranted outburst. 'I suppose I don't count for anything. I have done so much for you, George, but you can't even find time to fix my cupboards.'

The silence is broken by Candice.

'You mustn't be cross with my daddy. I'm sure he'll fix your cupboards soon, granny. Not so daddy?'

'Yes, my darling, daddy will fix granny's cupboards soon.'

The conversation for the rest of the supper is stilted and awkward. When they leave, Jane, who struggles with her own low self-esteem, thinks that she may have been the cause of Bessie's unhappiness, and asks George as they enter their home, 'Do you think it's because of me?'

'No, she had a bad day. I know my mother, she's very much an up and down moody woman. Today we caught her on the down.'

But George knows that it was precisely because of Jane that

his mother behaved so badly. He again decides to break the Thursday evening routine, and to wait on Bessie to make the invitation, should she so wish.

Chapter 18

A Strange Incident

With the weekend ahead, Jane and George abandon the idea of going to Margate and she asks him to accompany her to see a mime artist that she admires who is performing at the Alhambra Theatre. George is not a theatregoer and the only time he remembers going to see a live show was a Christmas pantomime that his mother had taken him to see as a child.

'Come on, George, I'll stand you.'

'No, no, I can afford the tickets, but I'm not sure what I'm letting myself in for. Wouldn't you rather go to the movies? There's *Lawrence of Arabia,* an exciting story of a British officer in World War 1...'

She looks at him with pleading eyes.

'And then he unites a bunch of Arabian tribesmen to take on the Turks, and then...'

Jane doesn't look impressed.

He sighs defeat. 'Okay, let's see your Marcel fellow.'

Despite his initial misgivings, George is mesmerized by the skill of the mime artist and thoroughly enjoys the performance. Coming out of the show they walk along the Berea Road pavement to where George had parked his car, when he catches sight of Derek coming towards them from the opposite direction. Derek is slightly unsteady on his feet but stiffens his back on recognizing George, who instinctively tightens his grip on Jane's hand as the adrenalin quickens the heartbeat and blood rushes to every defensive muscle and sinew.

'Shit! Look who's out on the street tonight!' Derek snarls with foul breath. He looks with steely eyes at Jane, but she quickly averts her gaze. He then approaches George in a threatening manner, pulling a knife from his pocket. The tension is electrifying. George stands his ground and stares him down. Jane tries to edge George away, but he releases her hand and braces himself for a violent confrontation.

Derek's eyes seem to change colour morphing into black holes of intense hatred. 'You bastard, you murdered my brother… in cold blood.'

'It was an accident.'

'Says who?'

'The court.'

'Fuck the court! I know what really happened,' he grunts, gesticulating with his knife. 'Yeah, I know!'

'How do you know? You weren't there. There were no witnesses.'

Derek is swaying on his feet and moves closer to George, who steps back from the point of the threatening blade. 'I have informers Georgie Porgie. So, I know that you deliberately killed my brother. It's time to get even.' He tries to attract Jane's attention, but she looks away. Then grabbing George by the jacket, he says accusingly, 'You pushed Buster out of the train,' and the blade narrowly misses George's chin. Derek laughs threateningly and jabs again with the knife. 'Not so?'

Jane is increasingly nervous about Derek's reckless emotional state and prompts George, 'Come, let's move on.'

Coming right up to Jane's face, Derek mockingly crows, 'Hello, sweetheart, are you sure this shithouse is not Peter?' Jane backs away from his foul breath. He then turns to the bystanders, shouting scornfully, 'This man's a fucking liar and a murderer.' People quickly walk away. Derek looks at Jane, 'Do you know why this prick wouldn't report the incident in the cemetery to the police? Because he was dealing in smuggled goods! Yeah, that's the sort of man he is. A fucking murderer, a liar and a smuggler.' He attempts to thrust the knife into George's chest but in his inebriated state he loses his balance allowing George the opportunity to wrest the knife from his hand and throw it into the gutter; he follows up with a devastating blow to Derek's jaw that sends him sprawling backwards.

'Stop it! Stop it!' Jane cries out, but to no avail. Although most theatregoers avoid the fracas a few gather around the two men who are swinging blows left, right and centre. A courageous young man steps into the fray to separate them.

'Hey! Come on now! Break it up, fellows! Now!'

Pointing an accusing finger at Derek, Jane shouts, 'That man's drunk!'

Several other men stand by ready to lend support. Derek looks at them with glaring eyes, rubs his chin, and moves away, pausing to give George a hateful glance. 'Watch your back, buddy boy. I'm not finished with you. Next time nobody will stop me.'

Jane gives George a tissue to hold against his bleeding nose. He looks to the man who broke up the fight, 'Thank you.' Jane takes George by the arm and leads him to her MG.

Although it's 11 o'clock, an hour past Bessie's normal bedtime, she is sitting at the front window seat and sees George being comforted by Jane as they walk towards their front door. Once inside Jane bathes his injuries in a solution of Dettol and puts Elastoplast on the open cuts.

George reveals the entire saga around Susan's death and that she had been involved in Derek's escort business. Jane listens uneasily, not wanting to make any judgment on the issue.

Feeling the need to justify his actions, he says, 'I honestly believe that Buster was somehow responsible for Susan's death, and I was going to do anything to find the truth, even if it meant changing my name.' He refers to the incident on the train and that a fight broke out between them and that's when Buster fell out of the moving train near Ladysmith. 'The court examined all the evidence and declared that I was not to blame for his death.'

Jane goes to bed that night with much on her mind, as he had spoken about that event before and she was disgusted to hear how he had thrown Buster off the train. Despite the lurid details, she begins to see George as a grieving husband who wanted justice for his wife.

The following morning, Sunday, she invites George to come with her to the local Baptist church.

'You need to explain all this to God.'

'What! Doesn't He exist everywhere? Can't I just do that here?'

'No, I want you to share your story with the pastor.'

'Never! That's no one else's business.'

'Well, just come with me and enjoy the singing. It will lift your spirit.'

More out of love and respect for her, George reluctantly attends the Sunday service, bringing Candice along too. He is moved by the sincerity of the congregation, many of whom reach out to him and Candice in friendship. He listens with half an ear to the sermon, which was on the parable of the prodigal son. He is surprised and impressed to learn how the aggrieved father could be so forgiving of his wayward son. But he had to get his head around the reaction of the good brother who had remained behind and worked tirelessly in the father's field, only to be considered as something of a Pharisee in the way he responded so self-righteously towards his delinquent younger brother. The parable made him think about the power of forgiveness, but he certainly can't see himself extending that to someone like Derek, whom he intensely hates and fears. It's only the moment when the pastor mentions the father putting a ring on the prodigal son's finger that George feels any direct connection with the story, and an impulse to do likewise with the beautiful woman sitting next to him.

On their way home, Candice puts herself between them, holding their hands and starts singing in her own comfortable pitch Eve Boswell's *Sugar Bush*.

Oh, Sugar Bush, I love you so

I will never let you go.
So, don't you let your mother know
Sugar Bush I love you so.

Jane gives her a loving smile, saying, 'My mom will be coming to Durban next weekend and she'll be staying at the Marine Hotel on the Esplanade. And my dad, too! I'm sure they'd love to meet you both.'

Chapter 19

Awkward Meeting

Remnants of British colonialism have stuck to the Durban landscape like pieces of stubborn English toffee, and many fine establishments have retained a colonial aura amidst uncharacteristic English weather. Tonight is a typical balmy, sub-tropical summer evening as George and Jane step out of their car in Gardiner Street and enter the imposing Marine Hotel that is the epitome of colonial splendour and practice. They pass through the inner, open courtyard where turbaned Indian waiters dutifully serve white guests sitting under miniature palm trees sipping cocktails and sundowners. Jane leads the way to room 250 where she knocks on the door to be received by an attractive middle-aged woman.

'Hello, Mom.'

George greets her with a warm smile, getting an instant snapshot of the woman's character and temperament.

'It's George, is it?' and stretches out her right hand.

He nods.

'You can call me Cynthia.'

George adopts a more formal manner on meeting the father. 'Good evening, Reverend Taylor.'

The minister throws back his head and laughs, 'I'm Gerald. You can drop the Reverend. It gives people the wrong impression. I'm no holy Joe.'

They move to the first floor and sit in an alcove outside the magnificent dining room to enjoy pre-dinner drinks. George sees a strong resemblance to Jane in the father but her fidgety fingers and tendency to be self-deprecatory appears to be mannerisms inherited from her mother. When asked her occupation, Cynthia replies that she is a helper in both the church and the wider congregation. Glancing at her husband, she smiles, 'Whether I'm any good at it… I'm not so sure.'

'My wife is a rock-solid support in my ministry. I couldn't function without her.'

George is very conscious about his language, and purposely avoids slang and zealously guards against any vulgar word slipping through his lips. He soon notices the close relationship between Jane and her father and the way he smiles and supports her points of view. In his easy-going manner, the Reverend has a way of putting people at ease, and says to George, 'I believe you are in the process of starting a new career,'

'Yes, I have sold my business and am now looking for a new avenue.'

'What are you good at?'

'I was trained at a technical high school and would be interested in something along those lines.'

'Have you thought of being an electrician?' Cynthia asks, giving George instant cold shivers, as the word electrician brings to mind his archenemy.

'I'm thinking of opening a small hardware shop in town.'

'Good luck to you,' Gerald replies.

They enter the gracious dining room and sit down to a sumptuous three-course dinner and a bottle of sparkling wine under a beautifully ornate, embellished white ceiling with decorative cornices. George is beginning to feel more relaxed in their company and hopes to make a sufficiently good impression to overcome any obstacles to their relationship. When the father says to him at the end of the meal that he hopes to see him again, he takes that as a positive sign. Jane confirms this by saying that he appears to have made a good impression on her folks.

'It's just a pity that Candice has the flu and couldn't come,' says Jane, adding, 'but I told them all about her in my letter.'

As he opens the passenger door to his car, he says, 'And, do they know that I love and want to marry you?'

Jane smiles awkwardly before replying, 'Not in so many words.'

George feels that he is still in limbo concerning his marriage proposal but is prepared to continue working at it.

As he turns his car turns into Gillespie Street, Jane nervously looks behind. George is aware of a dark blue sedan following them.

'I don't know if it's my imagination, but I think we're being followed,' he says.

George slows down, allowing the car to pass, but as it draws up alongside a masked gunman rises from the passenger seat. Jane quickly ducks her head under the dashboard. A gunshot rings out, narrowly missing George.

'Stay down,' shouts George, and puts his foot on the accelerator, racing straight ahead along Prince Street to the nearby police station, bringing the vehicle to a screeching halt. The tailing sedan is nowhere to be seen. George and Jane dash inside the police station causing instant consternation among the two officers manning the charge office.

'Hey, hey, hey! What's going on?' exclaims a young constable, expecting a dramatic scene to unfold.

'We've just been shot at,' Jane bursts out in fear.

'Okay, just calm down.'

His colleague rushes outside to look up and down the street but sees nothing suspicious.

'Two guys in a dark blue sedan… possibly a Mazda, followed us into Gillespie Street, and then opened fire from their passenger side window,' George tells them, still trying to control his breath and shaking hands.

'Did you get a good look at these guys?'

'Initially, I thought it was just one person behind the wheel, but when the car pulled up alongside us, a masked gunman rose from the passenger seat and shot at us,' George continues to explain.

'Any injuries?'

George shakes his head, while Jane replies, 'He must have missed us by millimetres.'

George glances at her, 'Well, it was actually me that the shot was aimed at.'

'Registration number?'

'All this happened so fast we were lucky to get away with our lives,' says George, hoping to calm down.

The policeman from the outside returns to the charge office.

'Nothing to report, Sergeant... except there's a bullet hole in your car, sir. I assume the blue Chevy Impala is yours?'

'Yes. You say only one hole?'

'That's all I could see.'

'Have you any idea who may be responsible?'

'Yes, I think I know who it was,' replies George.

The sergeant waits for a name.

George gives him Derek's name and the address of the electrical shop where he works. The sergeant takes a statement, gets George to sign it and gives him a reference number. 'We'll follow this up first thing tomorrow morning.'

'I don't think he works on a Saturday.'

'Leave it to us, we'll track him down.'

The police station is a short distance to George's maisonette where he leaves his car parked outside. Once inside, he pours two stiff whiskies for Jane and himself. Candice is spared the drama as she is spending the night with Bessie

Jane's head is in a spin and she holds her glass with trembling hands, looking to the whisky to calm her down. 'This fellow Derek is a danger to us. He must be locked up,' she says as if finally having a clear view of his character.

He looks askance at Jane. 'You don't have to worry about him.

It's my blood he's after.'

George is reluctant to reveal the full details of his earlier encounter with Derek at Smugglers as it may expose him to possible criminal charges. Jane puts on a romantic instrumental record that helps them relax. She sits next to him on the couch holding his hand. The music induces a soporific harmony and after a second whisky she surprises George by inviting him to share her bed. Although they've never had sex, she feels a deep maternal concern for his safety and wishes to comfort and console him. Neither of them immediately falls asleep so they spend the next few hours talking.

George releases suppressed feelings he had about Susan.

'You know what really hurt the most in my marriage to Susan?'

Jane waits for him to continue.

'The biggest disappointment was her betrayal. She really knew how to play the game. I obviously never fully understood her.'

Jane is silent as she too is hiding a liaison with a man that she doesn't wish to reveal… not at this stage, at least.

She quickly changes the subject.

'Tell me, George, what means most to you in life?'

'Well, at this stage, to give Candice the best I can afford.'

'That sounds very material.'

'My love for that little girl can't be measured in money. I want her to have a life that is true… that she can be proud of.'

'And you, what is the most meaningful thing in your life?'

'I'm not sure. At one stage I thought it was my faith because without that it would be like driving my MG in the dark. But today, I don't really know.' She turns her head the other way.

'Have you no long-term ambitions?' he asks.

'I have to sort out a few… a few problems before I can set my focus on that.'

She pauses.

'I just need time.'

'Well, in the meantime, is there anything you have in mind?'

'Yes, to avoid being shot at in the street.'

They burst out laughing which does much to relieve the tension of their recent dramatic event. A moment of silence speaks to their mutual desires to be united in a passionate gift of love. George, as a full-blooded male desperately wants to forge a lasting bond that will bring them closer, and she is beginning to have feelings for him that she had so assiduously tried to suppress. They are therefore not surprised to find in each other a deep desire for intimate contact and in this singular moment, their naked bodies melt as one.

Chapter 20

Masks

Early the following morning, Jane opens the front door to Bessie holding Candice's hand. The little girl breaks free and runs to Jane giving her a big hug around the legs while Bessie grimaces as she jealously views this spontaneous display of affection and tenderness.

'Is my son here?' she asks curtly.

'Yes, he's in the kitchen having breakfast. Do you want me to call him?'

'No thank you,' and she bustles her way through to the kitchen to be greeted by a sleepy George.

'Thanks for looking after Candice last night.'

'This is not to become a regular thing, I hope.'

'No, not at all! It's just that we had dinner with Jane's parents, and it was a chance for me to meet them.'

'Huh! While you go out gallivanting, I have to babysit. It's not good enough, George, I tell you!'

'It's not a regular thing, but if you're unhappy about it, I'll ask Agnes to stay behind, and she can sleep on the back porch.'

'You didn't look too good last night.'

'What do you mean? Were you spying on us again?'

'I happened to look out of the window when you got home and saw Jane leading you into the property. Were you drunk?'

George shakes his head. 'Bye Ma.'

Bessie turns to leave and sees Jane helping Candice to get dressed in her school uniform. She calls Candice to come and say goodbye. 'I can't now Gran. I'm getting dressed and will be late for school.'

'But it's Saturday.'

Jane interjects, 'Candice has been selected to be in the school's junior choir and they are rehearsing this morning.'

Watching Jane brush Candice's hair before putting on her white Panama hat, Bessie is jealous and upset that she wasn't told about this. Feeling ignored she storms out the house, slamming the door behind her.

After Candice is dropped off at school, George and Jane go shopping, but all the time he is aware of Derek's threats.

'There's no way you can approach him,' says Jane, after George suggests a meeting with the man.

'He's a dangerous criminal, George. He nearly murdered you. Leave it to the police.'

George is convinced that the gunman in the car was Derek, and the driver an accomplice, who might have been paid for his involvement. More light is shed on the incident that afternoon when Sergeant Reynecke calls round to update George on the case.

'We have arrested Derek Evans and charged him with attempted murder. He is being detained at Durban Central Police station until his bail hearing on Monday.'

'I hope you are going to oppose bail?' says George.

'That's our intention, but not our decision.'

'The magistrate can't let a maniac like that loose on the street,' declares Jane.

The sergeant shrugs his shoulders. 'By the way, we have found the perpetrator's vehicle. It was stolen and abandoned near the bottom of Point Road.'

'And the driver?'

'According to the statement made by Evans, the man was a seaman who, after abandoning the stolen car, boarded a ship which has since left port.'

'What a slimeball!' says George spitting the words out of his mouth.

George attends the bail hearing on Monday, and when Derek is led handcuffed into the courtroom, he can barely restrain himself from wanting to punch him. His bail application is denied, and he is remanded in prison until his trial in April.

Bessie phones to express her satisfaction with the court ruling; the call is answered by Jane who, on hearing her voice, calls George, but Bessie quickly interjects in a surprisingly sweet tone of voice, 'Hello, Jane, my dear, would you and George like to come around to my place this evening for supper?'

Jane can't understand this sudden change of attitude, but politely answers, 'Please speak to George first; if he's okay with it then I, for one, would love to come.

After George replaces the receiver, Jane turns to him with wide-eyed amazement. 'Is your mother bi-polar?'

'What do you mean?'

'One minute she's incredibly mean-spirited and the next she's as sweet as apple pie. I can't make her out.'

'Neither can I, but let's keep the peace and go.'

Winnie opens the door to George, Jane and Candice and a similar ambience to Jane's first visit is evident. Bessie is all smiles and cannot do enough to make her feel comfortable and welcomed. George takes his mother aside. 'Thank you, Mom, I appreciate what you're doing. I can't tell you how much Jane means to me.' He takes a big breath, 'I'm hoping...' He reads his mother's face anticipating something she isn't going to like hearing. 'I'm hoping she'll marry me so that we can create a happy home for Candice, and possibly have more grandchildren for you.'

Bessie turns away saying, as if she'd just eaten a dry corn cob, 'Come, I've baked a lovely honeycomb sponge pudding, which I know is one of your favourites.'

The evening continues without a hint of conflict, aided by the cheerfulness of Winnie, who is fond of telling stories about her nursing experiences. George and Jane leave holding hands, with Candice walking closely next to Jane.

'Well, that was a fine evening, what do you say?'

Jane smiles but ponders what lies behind the changing masks that Bessie wears.

Chapter 21

Things Fall Apart

A brisk southwesterly wind carries the notorious Durban pong from the whaling station on the Bluff across the popular seafront. It is early March and George closes the lounge window, puts on a face to match the unpleasant odour, saying, 'You're going to have to get used to this horrible smell from time-to-time until about September when operations at the whaling stations cease.'

'What on earth do they do with these poor animals?'

'Check your margarine in the fridge and the soap in the bathroom. It all comes from whale blubber.' Then, looking at her fair complexion, he adds, 'Also check your make-up... it could contain a little sperm.'

'What?'

'Spermaceti sperm... created in the head of a sperm whale,' he smiles.

'Thanks for the warning, I'll make sure my future cosmetics don't contain that stuff.'

'Then also check your cosmetic beeswax, because that's pure bee crap,' he laughs, enjoying the look of disgust on her face.

Jane clutches her stomach.

'What's wrong?'

'I've had these cramps on and off recently, but they seem to be getting worse. Kept me awake most of the night.'

'It's not er… you know?'

She utters a painful laugh, 'Pregnant! Me? No!'

'I was going to say… surely not after one night?'

'Nothing's impossible,' she smiles.

Apart from that one occasion, she and George still sleep in separate bedrooms and maintain a semblance of decorum insisted by Jane.

Touching her warm forehead, she says, 'I don't think I'm well enough to go to work today. A day's rest will put me right.'

George phones his mother to ask if she could pop in during the day to keep an eye on her, and to get any medicine she may need, adding that he aims to be home by 4.30 with Candice.

At about 9 o'clock. Bessie goes over to the house carrying a small shopping bag. Walking into Jane's room she senses an odour of vomit and almond.

'Shame, my dear, have you got an upset tummy?'

'Whatever it is, it's darn painful.'

'I hope it wasn't something you ate last night.'

'I don't know what it is. Perhaps it's my monthly. I've had terrible period pains in the past.'

'Do you want me to call a doctor?'

'No, that won't be necessary. I'll be fine soon.'

'Can I make you something to drink? Tea? Or, something cool?'

'Thank you, but you can bring me a glass of lime juice if you don't mind. You'll find the bottle in the kitchen.'

Bessie sends Agnes to the chemist to buy a box of disprin while she removes the plastic bucket next to the bed and flushes the contents down the toilet. She then goes to the kitchen to prepare the lime juice into which she adds several ice cubes and a powdered substance from her shopping bag. She puts the drink on the bedside table.

'Would you mind bringing the bucket back, I may need it later?'

Bessie replaces the bucket and offers Jane an oat cookie.

'Not just yet.'

'I'll leave a couple here on the table, should you feel peckish later. I made them fresh this morning.'

Agnes returns with the pills and is asked to clean the floor in Jane's bedroom. Jane swallows two disprin with lime juice, hoping to get some sleep. Bessie lingers a while. 'I'll be back before lunch.' She returns with a small flask in which she has prepared a drink for Jane. 'This should ease the pain, my dear,' she claims reassuringly. Bessie notices that the oat cookies have been eaten, and places more in the plate.

'How are you feeling, my dear?'

'I've still got these terrible tummy cramps, and a headache that is hard to shake off.'

'You must keep your strength up, my dear, by eating. I could do you a scrambled egg if you like.'

'Not just yet! I'll nibble away at the cookies.'

'If you change your mind about lunch, let me know.'

'I'm just thirsty. I could drink a gallon of water.'

'Let me get you some more juice, and I'll add some of my old mom's famous home remedy for period pains.'

Jane is looking pale and weak, and her speech is beginning to drag in pace and energy. Bessie returns with the drink and gets her to sit up by propping her back with pillows.

'The ice cubes are lovely.' Bessie feels her forehead. 'Yes,' says Jane, looking gratefully at Bessie, 'I'm feeling very feverish.' She drains the last drop to quench her thirst.

Bessie refills the glass, leaving it on the bedside table. She makes Jane comfortable before leaving the room and goes through to the kitchen to speak with Agnes.

'Don't give Jane any coffee or tea. She's taking disprin dissolved in water, so I'll leave this water bottle in the fridge. That's all she must have to drink until she's better. Call me, if it's urgent.'

'But today is my afternoon off.'

'That's fine. I'll be back before 1 o'clock.'

Bessie returns to bid Agnes goodbye. She looks in on Jane who is murmuring incoherently, closes her door and sits in the lounge to read the morning paper. She is startled by the sound of a thud. She opens the bedroom door to find Jane lying sprawled on the floor in excruciating pain. The bucket has overturned, and a stream of vomit is spreading out across the wooden floor. Bessie lifts Jane back onto the bed, cleans up the floor and prepares another drink for her.

'Help me... call a doctor... please,' Jane stutters the words out of her dry mouth. Bessie wipes her sweaty brow and gives her more liquid to drink. Jane continues moaning and soon lapses into a coma. Bessie closes the Bible next to her bed that was open with an underlined passage from St Luke's gospel.

'Whoever tries to save his life will lose it, but whoever loses his life for my sake will save it' (Luke 9:24).

She shuts the door and leaves the house to return home.

When George arrives with Candice just after 4 pm, he is thrown into a panic when he sees Jane lying unconscious on the bedroom floor struggling to breathe amidst an odour of vomit and bitter almond.

He calls his mother. She comes over and expresses an exaggerated look of alarm at what she sees. She starts wiping up the vomit while George, realizing the gravity of the situation, lifts Jane into his arms and carries her out to his car. Candice, who is crying, brings a clean blanket and wants to go with her daddy and Jane.

'No, stay here with granny, my love. Daddy must take Jane to the hospital straight away.'

Arriving outside Addington's casualty, he doesn't wait for a trolley but carries Jane into the emergency room where he pleads for immediate attention, telling a fussy nurse that he will fill in her forms later. A young doctor appears and instructs the nurse to wheel Jane into the examination room.

'What happened?' the doctor asks.

'I don't know. I came home from work and found her lying unconscious on the bedroom floor. She had complained in the morning of not feeling well. I really don't know. It might be something she had eaten that didn't agree with her.'

'Has she had any medication?'

'Not from a doctor as far as I know, as my mother was looking after her.'

The doctor shows George the door, 'Sorry, I need to examine her. Please wait outside.'

Before leaving George quietly pleads, 'Do whatever you can, please… just keep her alive… please.'

The admission's nurse thrusts a form into his hands. 'Fill this in, sir, it's compulsory.'

He finds this highly irritating but completes the form before the doctor emerges with a look of grave concern.

'Mr… sorry, what is your name?'

'Cooksley.'

'Mr. Cooksley, we are taking your wife into theatre as she appears to have consumed some or other poisonous substance. We suspect it may be cyanide, as there is a strong smell of bitter almonds in her breath.'

'She's not going to die, is she?'

He looks at George suspiciously. 'Please, be patient and let us do what we can for her. You'll find a comfortable waiting room near the operating theatre, so, take a seat, and we'll do the best we can to treat your wife.'

'She's not my wife, but a very special friend.'

He pauses a moment to say, 'If poisoning is involved, we are obliged to notify the police.'

'Yes, yes, do whatever you have to do. But please get her better.'

George goes to the public telephone to phone his mother to update her on the situation.

'Hello, my son, I've got Candice with me so don't worry about her. I'll prepare her supper and she can sleep over.'

'Look, I'm phoning from the hospital. Jane is in surgery. They are to give her a stomach pump. Can you shed any light on the matter?'

'Not really, my boy! I gave her disprin, which seemed to ease her discomfort… and she even slept for a while.'

'The doctor believes that she has eaten or drunk some or other poison.'

'Oh, how dreadful!'

'Did you notice anything strange about her condition?'

'Only that she complained of a severe stomachache, and I thought it was related to her period.'

'She wasn't feeling well in the morning.'

'Agnes got disprin from the chemist… but poison!'

'Yes, the doctor says there is a strong smell of bitter almond from her breath.'

There's a moment of silence before Bessie replies.

'Well, that's very strange! Where did she get that from, I wonder?'

'Anyway, take care of Candice as I'll be here until Jane comes out of surgery.'

'Of course, my son.'

About an hour later the doctor emerges from theatre to tell George that they had inserted a tube into her stomach to apply small quantities of liquid, which was then sucked out through the tube. He added that they were waiting for Jane to regain consciousness to do a bowel irrigation treatment.'

'What does that mean?'

'We'll administer an electrolyte solution until the rectal effluent is clear.'

George looks blank.

The doctor furrows his brow. 'So, you say, you have no idea how she could have ingested the poison?'

'No, we eat the same food and drink the same liquid… well, most of the time. And she was more or less fine the night before,'

'Do you think someone may have purposely poisoned her?'

'I can't think of anyone who'd have done such a thing.'

'As mentioned to you earlier, when we have suspicious circumstances such as poisoning, we are obliged to inform the police.'

'Yes, by all means, let them check out the premises to see that there is nothing there that she could have mistakenly taken, or… if there may be other causes.'

The doctor listens carefully while continuing to look at George suspiciously as if he is not revealing the full truth.

'May I see her now?'

'Only for a few minutes.'

The doctor accompanies George into the recovery room where he sees Jane looking as white as a sheet. Her eyes are still closed, but her breathing has improved.

'It's advisable not to touch her.'

'Why?'

The doctor merely shakes his head.

'You don't suspect me, do you?'

'We're not suspecting anyone at this stage. It was probably accidentally ingested. But we have to observe protocol.'

George whispers into Jane's ear. 'I love you… please… please get better.'

Jane makes a restless move with her head.

'She needs rest. We'll contact you the moment there is any change in her condition. You may return home or go back to the waiting room.'

'I'm not moving out of this hospital until you've told me that she's going to be okay.'

Chapter 22

Finger of Suspicion

The following day an inspector from the City Health Department arrives at George's maisonette to find only Agnes at home. She feels ill at ease with his authoritarian appearance and attitude, especially on telling her that he has instructions to inspect the premises for any possible poisonous substances. She takes him through to the kitchen where he checks all the contents of the various cupboards, taking samples of detergents, soap powders and ant poison. He then opens the fridge to check on foodstuff and liquids, opening and smelling the various contents. He takes samples of cooked chicken and meat and checks in the side door of the fridge to take additional samples of milk and water, including the water bottle that Bessie had left for Agnes to use for Jane, instead of tea or coffee. The inspector gets Agnes to sign for the selected items he has taken for laboratory testing, and leaves.

Later that same morning, George leaves the hospital after being told that Jane is out of danger. He goes straight to his mother's place to find her moving anxiously about in the kitchen. She's not expecting any callers and is surprised by his unannounced arrival. Quickly disposing of a brown paper packet in the dustbin, she turns to greet him with a fake smile.

'Hello George, you startled me! I didn't hear you come in.'

'I've come to tell you that Jane is out of danger.'

Bessie's pupils darken, 'Oh, really!' Again, forcing a smile, 'I mean, that's wonderful news.'

'Come, sit down and have a cup of tea with your old mother.'

She returns to the kitchen and George follows her.

'No, no, my boy, you sit down. I'll bring it to you. You must be exhausted being up all night.'

George is tired after a long, anxious night and enjoys the tea. He looks at his mother, the one person he has trusted throughout his life and thanks her for being with Jane.

'Did you not think to call the doctor when you saw her deteriorating situation?'

'Oh, I could see the poor woman was in a bad way... and that she wasn't getting any better. But... but she wouldn't hear of my calling a doctor.'

'You should've ignored that and called Dr. Weinberg.'

'Yes, I suppose so, but...'

'You know what Jane is like, she doesn't want to be a nuisance to anyone. Did she not mention the name of her own doctor?'

'No, no, not at all.'

'I really thought that the disprin would give her some relief, and... and when I saw her asleep, I didn't think it wise to wake her.'

George looks at her with disappointment.

'You know, sometimes women have discomforts... even pain during their periods... a lot of discomfort and pain, so I thought it was that... plus something she may have eaten,' she utters in a staccato pattern.

George pauses a moment, his mind fixed on the image of Jane lying in the hospital looking so vulnerable and weak. He refocuses on the present. 'I'll refund whatever you bought for her.'

'Not to worry, my pet, it was just a box of disprin.'

George rises to see if he can find something to eat in the fridge. Bessie follows him. He bends down to pick up a couple of raw almonds, which had fallen to the floor. She quickly snatches them saying, 'I was cleaning up when you came in.'

Somewhat taken aback, he replies defensively, 'I just need

to have something before I go on to work as we are still busy stocktaking and getting things ready for Edwards to take over.'

'Here, let me find you something.'

'What about a piece of the pudding you made for us… it was delicious!'

Bessie takes the pudding tray out of the fridge and cuts him a large slice.

George picks up a jug, 'I'd like some of this sauce.'

He puts his nose to it. 'Almonds… mmm… nice!'

'No, don't take that,' and snatches it from him. 'I was saving it for… for Winnie, she loves it.'

'And the cream?'

'Yes, help yourself.'

After snacking on pudding and cream, he moves to the front door where he turns to say, 'If you don't mind, could Candice and I have supper here again tonight?'

'Absolutely, my darling boy! Anytime.'

When George visits Jane that afternoon, he receives encouraging news that she is firmly on the mend and could be released in a couple of days. She is still very groggy and confused and unable to hold a steady conversation.

Over the next few days, George's mind is preoccupied with the responsibility of handing over his business and worrying about the woman he loves. When visiting her on the day of her release, she is dressed, packed and smiling as he enters the ward. He is especially pleased to see that she is fully compos mentis and slowly regaining her physical strength.

Back home, he goes out of his way to make her comfortable, saying how much she means to him and Candice, and that nothing like this must ever happen again. Jane refuses to lie in bed, preferring to sit in the lounge where she reads her Bible for short intervals between falling asleep in the chair. She had earlier noticed that her Bible, which she always keeps open next to her bed, had been closed, but doesn't think anything untoward except to say to George, 'I like to keep an open Bible next to my bed. It's like having the living word to speak to me.

It's a practice that my dad introduced in our manse in Pretoria where he had a Bible in our lounge opened on a new page every day, encouraging us to glance at a selected text to meditate on.'

He smiles and continues reading the evening news.

Jane continues, 'He believed in the power of the Logos, the Word made Flesh... and that, of course, is Jesus. He said that the words of the Bible have inspired more people in the world than any other book.'

George nods and moves to the sports page.

'When I was so desperately worried that I was going to die, I found a passage in St. Luke's gospel that had me thinking about death... and reading it helped to take away the fear of dying. It was the pain that I couldn't stand.'

George clears his throat. 'That's very consoling for you.'

The following day, George leaves instructions with Agnes on what to give her for lunch and says that should there be any problems she must call his mother immediately.

When he returns home with Candice at about 4.30, he sees Bessie in the lounge trying to persuade Jane to drink a glass of water. He hears Jane protesting that she doesn't like the taste of it, with Bessie insisting that it contains a healthy vitamin boost.

'I don't like it. It makes me feel sick,' Jane cries out in despair.

George bursts into the bedroom. 'Don't force her, Mom, if she doesn't want it.'

'I'm just trying to be helpful.'

Bessie takes the glass of water into the kitchen and pours it down the drain.

On returning to the lounge, George enquires, 'Where's Agnes?'

'I told her she could go off early, as she needed to do some shopping.'

Candice is delighted to have Jane back home, and holding out her Eskimo Pie says in her endearing voice, 'Do you want some of my ice cream, Jane?'

Jane takes a tiny lick and kisses Candice gently on the cheek.

'You shouldn't do that,' reprimands Bessie, 'you don't know what germs you could've picked up.'

'Oh, don't be silly, Ma. Candice is just trying to be kind.'

Looking increasingly agitated, Bessie snaps back, 'I don't like it. The child could fall ill.'

'I don't know what it is, but I seem to be getting the same symptoms I had earlier,' Jane utters pathetically, looking with despair at George, who replies, 'I'm here to keep a close eye on you, don't worry.'

She smiles.

He quickly adds, 'by the way, the City Health Inspector has taken samples of food and chemicals to see if there is anything in the house that could've caused your symptoms. I'm hoping we'll get the results soon.'

'These darn officials should be checking on the dirty kitchens of restaurants instead of worrying us,' says Bessie self-righteously.

'I'm glad they are checking on us,' replies George.

'Yes, of course… we need to get to the bottom of all this,' Bessie interjects, looking reproachfully at George, who picks up the telephone receiver to dial Dr. Weinberg's number. While he is talking in the background, Bessie says to Jane, 'I suppose these Health Inspectors have to earn their money. They'll always find something in your cupboard that isn't right. As far as I'm concerned, you've just picked up a virus or something that will soon wear off.'

George calls out, 'Dr. Weinberg will see you first thing tomorrow morning.'

'That's nice. Now, you must all have supper at my place again tonight,' says Bessie, trying to re-assert her authority.

Jane shakes her head, and looking at George suggests, 'Why don't you and Candice go?'

'Yes,' affirms Bessie, 'and you can take something back for poor Jane.'

'I like your cooking gran,' chirps Candice.

'Well, that settles it then. I'll see you two at half-past six.'

Bessie gathers her handbag and leaves through the front door.

'George, I don't know what your mother is putting in my water, but it tastes very bitter. She keeps telling me that it was an old trusted remedy of her mother or grandmother from the farm.'

George is aware of his mom's various home remedies and doesn't think anything of it.

'Have you eaten any food from outside of this house, something you may have bought at the tea room?'

'Not that I can recall.'

'Well, you've got the medication from the hospital to take in the meantime.'

'Your mother was very persistent, but I'm not going to have any more of her drinks, as I hate the taste of it.'

'What would you like for supper?'

'A scrambled egg will do fine.'

She clutches her stomach. 'These darn cramps!'

George comforts her by rubbing her back and arms.

'I'm not even sure that I want any food. I need to go and lie down. I'm feeling very weak again.'

George fetches her medicine and puts it on the bedside table together with a glass of clean water and her open Bible.

On the way to Bessie's house, a thought crosses George's mind, a thought that he quickly dismisses that perhaps his mother had given Jane something to eat and drink that could have been unintentionally poisonous... presumably done in error?'

Chapter 23

The Report

A health inspector in white safari suit stands in the lounge in front of George with a determined expression holding a file containing the laboratory report. He refuses the offer of a seat and delivers the toxicology report that leaves George in a state of shock. High levels of potentially lethal toxins were found in the sample of water taken from a plastic bottle in the fridge. Looking at George he says in a chilling tone of voice, 'The report has been sent to the Durban Central police station. They will be in touch.'

George swallows hard and is speechless.

'In the meantime, I have been requested by the police to make a thorough search of your premises to see if any of the substances found in the water are present in the house.'

George glances at Jane's bedroom door and moves to close it. This raises some suspicion with the inspector.

'I'm closing it as the person inside has just come out of hospital and is trying to catch up on lost sleep.'

'Is that the young woman who drank the poison?'

'Yes. But you mustn't upset her.'

'It's not my job to interview her I'll leave that to the police.'

He views George with increasing suspicion and scrutinizes every container in every cupboard before saying, 'I need to check what's in that room.'

'No, leave her alone.'

'Don't make my job more difficult Mr. Cooksley. The Police Station is not far from here.'

George opens the bedroom door and peers inside. 'If you tip-toe you can come in, but please don't wake her up.'

The Inspector removes the disprin and a glass of water from Jane's bedside table.

'You can't take the disprin away, she may need it.'

Again looking suspiciously at George, he affirms, 'Sorry, I'm just obeying orders,' and puts the box into his sample bag. 'There's a chemist at the corner should you need to buy more.'

Deep anger is building up towards this officious man, but George says nothing until he leaves the premises with the selected samples. George flops into the sofa, his head in a spin, trying to process what he has been told. He has to confront the terrible realization that his mother was attempting to murder Jane. He takes a deep breath before calling Agnes, who is outside hanging up the washing.

'Agnes…' His throat is so constricted with tension that he has to repeat, 'Agnes, come inside, I want to ask you a few questions.'

The woman enters the kitchen looking nervous and most distressed as she senses that something terrible has happened that could implicate her.

'Agnes… can you remember if my mother put anything in the water? The water she gave Jane to drink?'

Agnes needs a few seconds to answer. 'No, I saw nothing.'

'That's it? Nothing!'

'Your mother takes the water from the tap and gives it to Jane with the disprin. That's all I see.'

'Did you not see her put anything in the water after she took it from the tap?'

'No.'

'The water she put in the fridge… did you give any of that water to Jane.'

'Yes, Jane was thirsty, so I gave her that water as madam instructed.'

George looks distraught. 'Keep an eye on Jane, I'm going next door.'

He has lost all sense of restraint and with blind mechanical automaton, he bangs furiously on Bessie's front door. There is no answer. He bangs away again. George uses his duplicate key to enter. He shouts for his mother but receives no answer. He charges through the rooms, finding no one at home. He enters the lounge, lights up one of her filter-tipped cigarettes, breaking a firm undertaking he had made to give up smoking, but he needs something to calm his jagged nerves. He simply can't believe that his mother would attempt to murder Jane. There must be some other reason behind all this. His mind is in a spin. He hears footsteps approaching the front door. The Yale lock clicks open. Bessie enters carrying a parcel of groceries. She looks at George sitting in the semi-darkness of the room with the curtains drawn.

'Hello, my son, what are you doing here?'

George jumps to his feet, but words don't immediately fall from his lips.

'What's wrong with you, my son?'

'Did you poison Jane?'

He steps closer, confronting his mother face-to-face.

'Well, did you?'

All colour drains from her face. 'What a silly thing to say!' her voice breaking and her eyes rapidly blinking.

'Mother, I want the truth. Did you poison Jane?'

She turns away and moves towards the kitchen. 'I don't know what you're talking about.'

'I have seen the toxicology report. Jane was poisoned.'

'Poisoned! Oh, that's dreadful! Who would do such a thing?'

'You, mother! You! You put poison in the water you gave her to drink. And it's likely that you poisoned her the night we had supper here. Yes, the night when you were so nice to her!'

Trying to control her staccato delivery, she splutters, 'I think you should stop right there. How could you think such a thing? I am your mother. Have you ever known me to do such a terrible thing?' She dabs a handkerchief to her watery eyes.

George moves to the widow, trying to control his emotions. 'I'm not so sure about that.'

'What do you mean?'

He spins around, hitting his right leg with a clenched fist. 'Perhaps Susan didn't commit suicide after all.'

Bessie is shocked silent.

'Yes… perhaps you poisoned her too.'

Bessie is shaking almost uncontrollably, and her defensive anger comes to the fore. 'I've heard quite enough from you! Get out of my house at once! Go! Go back to that bitch you brought in from God knows where!' At the top of her voice, she yells, 'Go! Get out!'

George stubs out his cigarette with a hard stomp of his foot on her carpet, moves to the front door, turns on his heels, 'You'd better get yourself a good lawyer because you've got a lot to answer for.'

He slams the door on the way out.

Chapter 24

Getting Away

George is determined to move out of the house and get as far away as possible from his mother as if finally freeing himself from an infernal allergy. He is pleased to see Jane sitting up in bed, and, for the first time since the incident is once again smiling, a beautiful face framed within her long flaxen hair that had lost much of its sheen during her illness. He gives her a loving kiss and hug, saying, 'We're moving out.'

'Why? What's the rush?'

'I'll explain later, but too much has happened in this house for me to want to stay a minute longer.'

Giving George a penetrating look, 'I'm not waiting for an explanation. I want to know now what's going on.'

'My mother... yes, my dear loving mother, has been trying to... '

'Trying to what?'

'You won't believe it. I couldn't... but she tried to poison you.'

'Oh, my God!'

'Yes, she's insanely jealous of you. She's mad in the bloody head!'

Jane throws off the blanket and swings her legs across the bed, wanting to get up and get dressed.

'Wait, wait, wait,' he says, and sits down next to her holding her hand, saying soothingly, 'She must pay for what she's done.

I'm not sticking around here to give her any support... now, or ever again.'

'This is terrible! I can't believe it!'

'We'll find another place. I'll start looking today. Everything is ready for me to hand over the business to Edwards. So, there's nothing left to stop me.'

An intrusive sharp knock at the front door brings George to his feet. Agnes interrupts her cleaning of the lounge and opens the door to Sergeant de Villiers, a member of the Murder and Robbery Squad, who introduces himself and asks if this is also the address of Mrs. Jane Broadhurst, whose maiden name is Taylor. George overhears a male voice with an Afrikaans accent and moves to the front door. 'Good day, sir, I'm here to get a statement from Mrs. Jane Broadhurst.'

Jane is standing in the bedroom doorway listening. 'Yes, I am well enough for that.'

After Jane has given a detailed explanation of events leading up to her hospitalization, the sergeant turns his attention on George.

'Mr. Cooksley, would you mind coming with me to Durban Central as we need to ask you a few questions?'

Jane clutches George's hand.

'He has nothing to do with my illness. Speak to his mother.'

'We will be speaking to everyone that we believe can help solve this crime.'

'Don't worry, Jane, I want this matter cleared up as much as anyone else.'

George leaves with the policeman, saying, 'If I'm delayed, please ask Agnes to pick up Candice.'

Meanwhile, Bessie has phoned her sister, Winnie, telling her of the terrible accusation levelled at her by George. Winnie swiftly makes her way to her sister's house, finding her in tears.

'I can't believe my George would say such a terrible thing to his mother.'

Winnie fusses about trying to pacify Bessie, 'Don't worry, my dear, it will all come right.' She goes to the kitchen to make tea, all the time stressing that there is nothing to worry about. 'Jane must have eaten or drunk something somewhere... but not here. Not at your house, Bessie, never! I'll vouch for that! Never, never, never!'

'George accused me of poisoning the water I left for her to drink.'

'What nonsense! Maybe, Agnes put something in it. She could've had a grudge against the woman, or was possessed by the *tokoloshe.* You never know!'

'I can't stay here if George is going to be so horrible to me.'

'Then, come and stay at my place.'

She kisses Winnie on the forehead. 'My dear sister... always willing to give a helping hand.'

At Durban Central, George is led into the interrogation room where he encounters Detective Marais, a stern-faced individual with no age lines around the mouth suggesting that he is not an individual accustomed to smiling. He keeps George standing for several minutes before telling him to sit down, and then stares him down with a threatening gaze.

'Mr. Cooksley, we found a bottle of water in your refrigerator that was mixed with traces of cyanide. Can you explain this?'

George cannot bring himself to say that he thinks his mother is responsible. 'I have no idea who contaminated that water.'

'Was it your bottle?'

'No.'

'Then to whom did the bottle belong?'

'My mother.'

'Your mother!'

'She had been nursing my sick girlfriend.'

'So, are you suggesting that your mother poisoned your girlfriend?'

He cannot give a straight answer. 'Not intentionally.'

'What do you mean?'

'Perhaps someone else may have added the poison...'

'Who?'

'I have no idea.'

'Then how?'

'The water may have somehow got contaminated.'

'By itself?'

George shakes his head.

'Are you sure it wasn't you?'

'I love Miss Taylor and would never hurt her.'

Marais takes down copious notes. 'We have yet to speak to your maid... what is her name?'

'Agnes Dlamini.'

'And to your mother, but that doesn't put you in the clear. So, in the meantime, you are free to go, but you are to check-in at the Point police station every day until further notice.'

Sergeant de Villiers drives him home, drops him off, and goes next door to speak to Bessie. But there's no answer to his persistent knocking. As he turns to go, a woman carrying a suitcase is seen leaving from the back entrance.

'Excuse me, lady!' he shouts.

But Bessie hurries towards a parked car, gets in and is driven away by Winnie. De Villiers jumps into his vehicle and pursues them down Prince Street. But Winnie knows all the side streets and back alleys in the area and ducks into a dark driveway where her car remains undetected. She waits fifteen minutes, before reversing out to make her way to her nearby flat. Bessie's heart is thumping ten to the dozen, but she is relieved to have escaped.

'I can't stay with you, Winnie. The police will soon trace me here.'

Winnie looks deeply into her sister's eyes. 'Oh, God, Bessie! What have you done?'

'I know a place in Pretoria where no one will bother me.'

Bessie searches Winnie's cupboard for something strong to drink.

'Here, let me pour you a stiff brandy.'

They sit down in the lounge, but Bessie cannot relax and is constantly fidgeting. Winnie is beginning to doubt her sister's innocence, and her mind casts back several months earlier when she gave Bessie a box of pills from Addington.

'Bessie... I'm just curious to know about those methadone tablets I gave you... you didn't perhaps mix them with the disprin you gave Susan... did you?'

Bessie's face turns white, and her eyes blaze fury. 'Are you also now accusing me of Susan's death?'

Winnie swallows hard. 'I don't know what to think.'

'You know what I wanted those tablets for. I crushed them and put them into pieces of bread to get rid of the rodents. That's what I did, nothing else.'

'Yes, yes, of course, Bessie, because you didn't want to waste money buying rat killer.'

Bessie takes a big gulp of brandy.

'Come to think of it though, you could have used bicarb of soda... and those rodents would've just popped themselves to death.'

'Oh, don't be bloody stupid, Winnie! Popped to death! What are you talking about?'

'Listen, I'm trying to help you, but I don't want to be involved in any funny business.'

Bessie slams down her empty glass, stands up, demanding, 'Take me to the railway station. I'll send you a forwarding address... where to send my other stuff. Sell the furniture and keep the money.'

'How will you survive?'

'I've got my fixed deposit and other savings to live on.'

'But what about the house?'

Bessie ponders the question before replying. 'I'll have to think about that. I'll let you know.' After a brief pause, she lightens up with an answer. 'Why don't you move in there? Could save you flat rental.'

Winnie drops her off at the main station where she books a coupè compartment on the Trans-Natal Express.

Chapter 25

The Investigation

Police arrive at Bessie's residence with a search warrant. They bang furiously on the door threatening to break it down when George comes across with a duplicate key. Detective De Villiers accompanies detective Marais and several other officers, who begin a thorough search of Bessie's home and belongings. George is told not to interfere, and he lingers briefly in the lounge, where a familiar stale smell of *eau de cologne,* Mr. Min Furniture Polish and cheap plastic tablecloths permeates the closed environment. De Villiers finds the smell nauseating and throws open the windows. George feels depressed and can't stand to be in the house another minute; he gives Marais the duplicate key and leaves.

Meanwhile, detergents and aerosol canisters are put in a cardboard box together with items from the fridge, including a plastic bottle of water, as well as a variety of tablets and medicine from the bathroom's vanity cupboard and bedroom dressing table. Detective Marais finds a half-empty packet of raw bitter almonds at the back of the kitchen cupboard and that too is taken away for laboratory testing.

As the police team is about to leave, Detective Marais sees a strange-looking man, wearing corduroy trousers with bicycle clips clamped to the ends of the trouser legs, enter the house. Marais steps forward authoritatively saying, 'Sorry, sir, this is a police investigation, you can't enter these premises.'

Charlie is stunned.

'It's a possible crime scene.'

'Hells bells! Crime scene! Where's Bessie Cooksley, the woman who lives here?'

'That's what we'd like to know.'

'Sorry, sir, we are very busy. But… er… what is your association with Mrs. Cooksley?'

'She's a friend. I've known her for years.'

Marais takes down his details. 'Thank you, we'll be in touch.'

Charlie hurriedly exits and runs up the steps to George's front door, where he bangs away until an exasperated George opens it.

'For stuff's sake, Charlie, what's up?'

'That's what I want to know. Next door is crawling with coppers.'

'Come inside.'

George offers Charlie a beer and then outlines the whole saga that implicates his mother in the crime.

'Shit a brick, George! I never thought that of your old ma.'

'Well, we don't know anything for sure. But her running away points to a very guilty woman.'

'Look, if there's anything I can do to help, just let me know.'

'At this stage, relax! It's in the hands of the police.'

Charlie finishes his beer and hints at a second, but George indicates that he has to go out.

'I'll give Win a call… or, better still, I'll go and see the old wench for an update.'

'All info would be helpful. Anyway, thanks for the visit,' and he shows Charlie to the front door. Charlie hops onto his old Chooks and pedals away furiously down Prince Street as if doing the final stretch of the Tour de France.

When George picks up Candice from nursery school later that afternoon, he is distressed to hear her say that she doesn't ever want to go back there.

'Why my sweetheart?'

'Because they say my granny is a bad woman.'

'Don't listen to them… don't listen to anyone who says that about your gran.'

'But where is granny?'

'Granny's not well. She has a problem,' he replies, pointing to his head. 'She can't think clearly and has gone away to get better.'

'My friend says granny puts nasty things in peoples' food.'

'Where does she get that from, I wonder?' and lifting her into his arms, adds, 'some people talk a lot of nonsense. But remember, no matter what anyone says or does, your daddy loves you, and will always protect you.'

On arriving home, Candice runs into Jane's room but finds it empty. 'Where's Jane?'

'She's gone for a walk on the beach with Agnes.'

George feels that his world is falling apart but is pleased to be at home now that the business has been sold, leaving him time to plot his future. He knows that children can be very cruel with their taunting and nasty comments, making him more determined than ever to pack up and move away.

When George sees Agnes return alone, he blurts out, 'Where's Jane?'

'She told me to go back to the house because she wanted to be alone.'

'Where did you leave her?'

'On the beach… in front of the Model Dairy.'

He hurriedly makes his way down to the beachfront where he sees Jane sitting alone on the sand staring out over an expansive cobalt blue ocean. She is locked in thought and doesn't notice his presence until he sits down next to her, putting his arm around her. They remain silent for some time before she says, 'I'm going home.'

George is stung silent for a moment.

'I can't stay with you.'

He is thrown into confusion but offers a sympathetic response, 'Perhaps that's a good idea. You need to get some rest… and get yourself completely better before coming back.'

There is a long pause before she replies, 'I'm not coming back, George.'

He swallows the word 'Why?' making it barely audible.

'I'm no good to you or Candice. I can't be what you want me to be.'

'But I just want you to be yourself.'

'It's no good George. I've brought you misery. It's me, I know.'

She looks into his eyes, 'I'm a fake.'

'What do you mean?'

'Everything about me... when I stepped onto your showroom floor, I presented myself as a glamorous woman. But that wasn't me. I'm not that person. Never was!'

'That's fine by me. We all role play at times, trying to be someone else. So, what!'

She lowers her gaze. 'You don't understand... I am no good for you... and I was certainly no good for your mother.'

'My mother did an evil thing... and she must pay for it.'

'If I wasn't in your life, it wouldn't have happened.'

'Jane, listen, I want you in my life. I need you in my life... and so does Candice.'

She clasps George's hand. 'I'm very fond of you... I really am.'

'Fond? Is that all?'

'I do love you... but...'

She can't find the words to adequately express her feelings for him. 'I love you too, but I'm not in love... and that's the difference.'

'I don't care. Love... fondness... friendship... that's good enough for me.'

'It's not George. You deserve better, and I can't offer you that.'

George drops his head in despair. 'I am far from being the best that I can possibly be. So, if anyone should be putting themselves down, it's me.'

She looks at him quizzically.

'I haven't told you this. In fact, I haven't told anyone this, but I am far from being the good man you think I am.'

She remains silent allowing him space to continue.

'I left a man to die... a man whose life I could possibly have saved. But I wanted him dead. I caused his death.'

'What are you trying to tell me?'

George gives her a truthful account of the death of Buster, which was intentional and without remorse. A deathly shadow veils her face with flash-back memories of identifying Buster's corpse, and her immediate response to side with Derek in avenging his brutal death.

Jane feels trapped but doesn't confess her relationship with Derek. She drops her gaze looking increasingly despondent.

'Derek has tried twice to kill me but, so far, I've managed to escape.'

Jane distractedly picks up a shell and breaks it in half, pushing both pieces deep into the sand with her foot. If she were truthful, she would have to confess that she has fallen in love with George but cannot tell him because she believes that he would never forgive her for lying and betraying his trust.

'The first time that Derek tried to kill me I managed to duck into a church... next to a graveyard.'

Jane tries to lighten up by replying with a forced smile, 'I suppose that's one way of God getting you to visit Him.'

'Strange you should say that because I got a real sense of... how should I say... of an unseen presence in that church. I was sitting under a red glowing lamp near the altar of the Emmanuel Cathedral.'

'A red, glowing lamp! We don't have anything like that in our church.'

'A priest told me it was to indicate the true presence of Jesus in the tabernacle.'

She looks at him askance. 'Did you believe him?'

'I'm not a religious man. I don't go to any church, so I can't confess to believe in anything, but I sensed the power of peace there. It was all around me... I could almost touch it. I had never experienced anything like that before.' He shrugs his shoulders. 'That's all I can say.'

The rising tide with its waves crashing relentlessly along the shoreline begins to intrude on their space forcing them to get up.

Isolated in their own worlds as they grapple with deep-seated issues, they head for home leaving the sea to wash away their footprints on the shifting sand and dissolve all dreams of a future together.

.

Chapter 26

Settling Issues

Today, May 15, is George's 29th birthday but he faces a bleak celebration without Jane and his mother. But at least he has a loving daughter, Candice, whom he sets out to make the princess of his special day. He takes her to the Kenilworth Amusement Arcade along the central beachfront where they enjoy dodgem car rides and other fun-filled moments. He tells her that she is entering a very exciting world where men are now flying through space, sharing the news about the Mercury-Atlas 9 American space mission, crewed by the astronaut, Gordon Cooper. But by the end of the day, he feels desperately lonely and if he could crawl into a space capsule and orbit the earth to get away from his depression, he would do so gladly.

With winter brooding over the land people are preparing for the coming cold months, except for Durbanites, who are fortunate to enjoy temperate winters that are shared with many upcountry visitors who flock *en masse* to the city during its winter holiday season.

During this depressing time in George's life, police continue to call around asking about his mother and her whereabouts, but no one claims to know where she is, and those that do have sealed their lips. Winnie hasn't shared all she knows with Charlie, but even she is not sure where Bessie is currently staying, except somewhere in Pretoria. Soon after her arrival, Bessie made contact with a spinster cousin who lives in a flat in Sunnyside, but then she disappeared soon afterwards and is believed to be living in the working-class suburb of Proclamation Hill.

It's Friday mid-morning, and Bessie is standing in front of a mirror in a hairdresser's salon in Pretoria West admiring her new blonde persona. She turns to view her profile and proffers a smile that only she can appreciate. She angles the opposite profile and stretches her sagging gooseneck while considering herself to be quite attractive for someone her age. Subconsciously, she thinks that as her son likes blondes, he may be more forgiving and soften his attitude towards her, though in reality, she knows there is scant chance of that happening. She returns to her remote and run-down boarding house in Proclamation Hill, where she hopes to remain incognito.

She has checked in as Mrs. Barbara Baxter, claiming to have come from Springs where she had lived with her husband until his death. Although the owner of the boarding house and other guests are Afrikaans-speaking, she can understand the language and gets by with basic communication that includes words of both official languages.

Although she has gone to great effort to change her appearance and identity, she is not coping with the deep depression that has gripped her mind. When looking at herself she feels as if she is staring into a vacuum and contemplating an empty future. While not regretting anything she has done, not even poisoning Susan and attempting to kill his new girlfriend, she nevertheless feels wretched for having destroyed a precious mother/son relationship.

She is wracked in misery, guilt and self-hatred as she fully registers the loss of George in her life. He had always been at the centre of her world. And now she can't imagine life without him. She also misses her sister, Winnie, and little Candice to whom she was hoping to become a surrogate mother. She starts self-medicating with over-the-counter anti-depression tablets and also visits a local doctor, who prescribes stronger antidepressants, but nothing she takes relieves her deep, incipient misery. She further isolates herself from society, knowing that if she becomes too visible, she stands a chance of being arrested, and, if Jane's body is exhumed, a coroner could well report traces of arsenic in her hair and elsewhere, thereby charging her with first-degree murder. The strain of all this is taking its toll and Bessie believes the time has come for action.

Meanwhile, back in Durban, George's plans for the future have gone awry and he feels lost without Jane, who left to return to her parents in Pretoria. Candice is now the sole focus in his life, and he aims to make her future as secure and happy as he possibly can. Although his mother owns the maisonette, preventing him from selling it, he has managed to let the two semi-detached dwellings to tenants. He packs up the remains of her personal belongings, which Winnie has taken to her flat, while the furniture that neither of them nor Charlie wants, is sold. George manages to wrap-up the entire process in six weeks before finding a medium-sized house in Wadley Road, Umbilo, close enough for Candice to attend the nearby Penzance Primary School where she is to be enrolled the following year in Grade 1. Furthermore, he finds a small hardware shop in West Street that he buys, intending to build it into a bigger concern. But he is not finished with the law, because he has been subpoenaed to appear in court in the trial of Derek Evans. He gathers that Jane has also been called to give evidence and is looking forward to a reunion.

George takes the witness stand on the first day of the trial and looks around the courtroom but doesn't see her. But as he is describing the events of that evening, he notices her entering the courtroom where she is directed to a seat. He is momentarily distracted until the prosecutor demands his full attention.

'Sorry, I was … er, just…'

The prosecutor glares at him. 'We need to go back to an earlier incident when you had a fight on the Trans-Natal Express with the brother of the accused because we believe that incident has a direct bearing on the recent incident when Mr. Derek Evans is alleged to have tried to kill you.'

The prosecutor takes a moment to gather his papers before continuing, giving George the chance to take another peek at Jane.

'Your description of the incident on the train correlates with the statement you gave afterwards to the police in Ladysmith, but my question to you Mr. Cooksley is this...' He starts tugging at the edges of his black gown. 'Why do you think Mr. Derek Evans wanted to kill you?'

'Revenge.'

'Address the judge, not me.'

'Revenge, your honour! Mr. Evans believed that I was responsible for his brother's death.'

The judge leaning forward frowns, 'Well, were you?'

George is stunned silent for a moment.

'Answer the question,' the imperious judge demands.

'All this was cleared up, your honour, by an earlier court decision that found there was insufficient evidence to charge me with culpable homicide. It was an accident... yes, an accident when the deceased and I were involved in a drunken brawl and...'

'And then?'

'Mr. Buster Evans complained of being hot and opened the carriage door to stand in the opening. He then took a step down to the top of the coach's steel steps to cool off.'

'All this time while the train was moving?'

'Yes, your honour.'

'He then threw open his arms shouting an obscenity... and lost his balance. I tried to pull him back inside the carriage, but then we both lost our balance and fell backwards, with him hitting his head on the rocky ground.'

George pauses briefly.

'Carry on Mr. Cooksley,' prompts the judge.

'Mr. Evans, unfortunately, struck his head against a rock... and subsequently died.'

'But his twin brother Derek doesn't appear to agree with that finding, does he?'

'I can't help that.'

'Mr. Derek Evans believes that you were implicated in his brother's death... because you had a motive... a very strong motive, Mr. Cooksley. And that motive, according to Mr. Derek Evans is that your wife was having an affair with his brother. Not so?'

George sees Jane sitting at the back of the courtroom, wishing somehow that she could cover his sense of shame and humiliation.

'Answer the question.'

'Yes, he had an affair with my wife, but that was not the cause of the fight.'

'You say his death was accidental?'

'Yes.'

'But how is it that both of you were on the same train and in the same compartment?'

'That you must ask the clerk at the railway's ticket office. I had no idea that the man I was initially drinking with was the same person who had an affair with my wife.'

The judge interjects. 'The fact that no witnesses came forward in that hearing, no culpability could be found on Mr. Cooksley's part, and the case was closed.'

'Yes, I am aware of that, your honour, but what I want to establish is whether the deep animosity between Mr. Cooksley and the deceased and the deceased's brother, Mr. Derek Evans, could explain the shooting incident.'

As George continues his testimony, his eyes lock on Derek's who is sitting in the dock staring daggers at him. 'As I said, your honour, it was revenge based on erroneous assumptions that Mr. Evans had about my involvement in his brother's death.'

'Thank you, Mr. Cooksley, you may step down.'

After this ordeal, George takes a seat in the courtroom and waits to hear Jane's evidence. She is looking so beautiful and vulnerable, with George feeling so isolated from her life.

'I gather you were in the front passenger seat of the car the night of the shooting.'

'Yes, sir.'

She looks across to Derek.

'Describe to the court what you saw.'

'Mr. Cooksley was driving down Gillespie Street in his Chevy sedan and I was sitting next to him. It seemed to be a perfectly normal Friday evening with perhaps more traffic and people out and about than usual. We noticed that a dark, navy blue car was following us. The car then began to slowly overtake us. At the point where it drew parallel with our front window, a masked figure rose up from the front passenger seat, and I saw a revolver appear at the window, followed by a gunshot. It all happened so fast.'

'Were you or Mr. Cooksley injured in the incident?'

'No, we were lucky to escape injury.'

'Then what did you do?'

'We sped away and reported the incident to the nearby Point Police Station.'

The prosecutor asks, 'Can you identify the man who fired the shot? Is he sitting in this court?'

Jane takes a cursory glance at Derek.

The prosecutor points at Derek. 'Was it him?'

'No, the man who fired the shot was wearing a balaclava.'

'And the driver? Did you see who that was?'

Her heart is pounding, but she nervously raises her right hand pointing at Derek, who gives her a look of intense hatred.

'Are you sure, Ms. Taylor?'

'Positive.'

Derek mouths words that she thankfully cannot hear.

'Thank you, Ms. Taylor, you may step down.'

After giving her evidence Jane sits next to George to hear Derek's side of the story.

Following the prosecutor's outline of the events of the evening of the shooting, Derek's defence advocate says that some important aspects of the case are purely circumstantial and uncorroborated and that there is no evidence to put his client at the scene of the crime.

The prosecutor snaps back. 'You presumably didn't hear the clear statement made by Ms. Taylor. She has positively identified the driver as Mr. Derek Evans.'

Derek looks crushed. The prosecutor continues, 'We have the weapon and the ballistic tests to prove that the calibre bullet used in the crime came from that revolver, which is exhibit-A. We have fingerprints, but the masked individual in the car is believed to have fled the country and we are unlikely to secure extradition. The car had been stolen, and there is every reason to suspect that the revolver had also been stolen.'

The defence advocate looks accusingly at George saying, 'Mr. Cooksley sells second-hand cars and must have made enemies, besides my client. There could well have been a disgruntled customer behind that balaclava. And the driver could well have been someone who looks like my client. We simply don't know. Therefore, we have no proof that it was Mr. Derek Evans.'

When Derek takes the stand, he strongly denies being the driver and says it is a conspiracy theory given to the police by George because he knew that his ex-wife was an escort who had had sex with many other men, including himself and his twin brother. George is enraged when he hears this but can do nothing to counter the accusation. The court is adjourned for the day, and, with no further witnesses to be called the judge says he will hand down judgment the following morning. Jane, who sat nervously throughout Derek's testimony, is invited by George to stay overnight at his new home in Umbilo. She reluctantly accepts. Candice is thrilled to see her and gives her a tight hug around the legs.

George makes no further attempt to express his deep feelings for Jane, instead enjoys her warm and loving company.

'You were quite nervy during the trial,' he says to her.

'That man gives me the creeps.'

He and Jane finish off a bottle of wine, as both wish to put this business behind them.

The following morning, they return to the court to hear

judgment. Derek's advocate stands to request permission to make a final statement to the court. The judge hesitates for a moment before allowing it. The six-foot-tall advocate makes a striking impression as he boldly states, 'There is absolutely no evidence to put my client at the scene of the crime, other than the statement made by Ms. Taylor. And what she claims to have seen must be dismissed, as it was nighttime where reduced lighting would automatically place her evidence in doubt. Furthermore, my client reliably informs me that Ms. Taylor worked for him as an escort and they had had a close relationship. It was she who identified the body of my client's brother.' The advocate looks accusingly at Jane.

George can't believe what he is hearing and instinctively shifts his body away from Jane's. 'But now, your honour, Ms. Taylor is so bewitched by her new boyfriend George Cooksley that she can't see straight. The court must, therefore, dismiss her evidence as highly suspect and questionable.'

There is general murmuring throughout the court and all eyes descend on Jane. She gets up and hurries out of the courtroom. George sits ashen-faced.

'Furthermore, your honour, the court should take into consideration the deep animosity the victim has towards my client. He would do anything to implicate him in any way possible to destroy not only his reputation but also his life.' He concludes by saying, 'to convict my client of attempted murder would be a great miscarriage of justice.'

The judge declares a recess until after lunch.

George walks out of the Supreme Court building in a daze. He finds an eatery in one of the nearby arcades where he has a coffee. His mind is in turmoil. He can't believe that Jane was a deliberate plant right from the beginning, sent by Derek to spy on him and could have been aware of plans to murder him. He takes a long, meandering walk along the city's pavements until the court proceedings resume at 2 pm.

In his judgment, the judge says an attempt to portray Derek as the innocent victim would be a travesty of justice. Not only did the woman who had known him intimately, identify him but his fingerprints had been found on the steering wheel of the abandoned car.

'Mr. Evans had a strong motive to kill George Cooksley, that is undisputed. It was the death of his twin brother that drove the accused to seek revenge.'

He pauses briefly.

'I find no extenuating circumstances in this case, and therefore find the accused guilty as charged.'

Derek drops his head in defeat. Loud murmurings break out, needing the judge to bang his gavel firmly on the desk to bring the court back to order. 'Will the accused please stand.' He clears his throat. 'Derek James Evans, this court finds you guilty of the attempted murder of George Cooksley and sentences you to 12 years imprisonment.'

The defence advocate shakes his head, and turns to Derek, mouthing, 'We'll appeal.'

George returns home to find Jane packed and gone. Agnes says that she didn't even say goodbye.

George sits out in the garden where he had recently started planting a bed of roses in Jane's honour. He had planted two new varieties, one that he called the Beauty Rose and the other, the Love Rose.'

A sad smile creases his face as he recalls saying to her, 'When you look on those roses, I shan't ever need to tell you that you are beautiful.'

He hears a sniffle and turns around to see Candice standing on the front step of the veranda crying.

Chapter 27

New Dimensions

Candice proudly finishes her sandcastle on the beach, placing a small blonde lady doll on top of the main tower. She crawls on her knees around the moat reinforcing its battlements when a fat little girl comes running past and tramples down the tower. Candice screams at her, but she laughs rudely and keeps running. George, who sitting in his bathing trunks on a deck chair nearby, shouts at the *enfant terrible*, who is promptly stopped by her mother and dragged back to apologize to Candice. 'I'm terribly sorry,' the embarrassed young mother says, looking shame-faced. 'She just gets out of hand at times.'

Candice is in tears and doesn't wish to look at the woman or her little brat. 'Say sorry to the little girl,' the mother demands.

'No.'

'Say sorry, or there'll be no ice cream for you.'

The little girl drops her gaze, and mumbles, 'Sorry.'

'You, horrible monster!' Candice cries out bitterly.

'Candice! That's not a nice way to speak,' and George looks ruefully at the woman, saying, 'My daughter's going through a bad patch at the moment.'

The little fat girl kicks sand at Candice prompting her mother to pull her away and retreat. Candice runs into the arms of her father.

'That was Jane's castle, daddy.'

'Yes, sweetie pie, I know.'

'When is Jane coming back?'

George wishes a huge wave would wash over him and wake him up from this horrible nightmare. He gets out of the deck chair cradling Candice's head against his strong shoulder, wishing that he could shield her from any more emotional trauma. In his wretchedness, he mumbles, 'I don't know when she's coming back, my love.'

'Can we fetch her?'

'I don't think so.'

'Why can't I have a mummy?'

George gathers their belongings, and they make their way off the beach. He keeps telling himself that Jane's deceit and betrayal can't be true and builds a confusing barrier of resentment and hatred towards her.

Despite these persistent and agonizing memories, George has important business to conclude and he makes an appointment to see his lawyer. Although he knows that he cannot take ownership of his mother's property until such time that she is found, and some agreement is reached between her and the authorities he is advised that the rental income would continue to be paid into the lawyer's trust account.

Leaving the lawyer's office in lower Smith Street he begins walking part of the way home, wanting to clear his mind of the accumulated damning memories. On passing Emmanuel Cathedral, he decides to go inside, and once again he sits near the glowing red lamp in the sanctuary, a place where he had previously found serene tranquillity and peace of mind. His eyes are drawn to the tabernacle where the priest had told him resides the true mystical presence of Jesus Christ. He has no understanding of any of its theology but imbibes the cool, silent atmosphere of this 19th-century cathedral. His eyes drift upward to a carved Carrara Marble cross, a gift from Empress Eugenie, wife of Napoleon III of France, following the death of her son in the Anglo-Zulu War of 1879.

Hanging from the beams is a large and daunting crucifix with the body of a dying Christ. The word Judas springs to mind, not because of its Biblical significance but because it's a common name for a traitor like Jane. He agonizes over her betrayal and deceit. Yet, she also betrayed Derek as her evidence led to him being put away for 12 years. George tries to make sense of all this confusion and hopes the stillness of his surroundings will infuse a measure of meaning and peace.

In his deep reflection, he is reminded of the many wrongs that he has committed throughout his life, particularly those that have occurred recently. He realizes that leaving Buster to die on the side of the railway track and ignoring his desperate pleas for help was gravely wrong. He had deliberately plotted to kill him and has shown no remorse. He lied under oath in court about that incident. In the eyes of the law, he is guilty of perjury and premeditated murder. He accepts that he may be forced to carry that burden for the rest of his life. Many other wrongful acts float to the surface of his consciousness, as well as the many shameful deeds he has suppressed over the years – his moments of pride, arrogance and anger that hurt other people, either in word or deed. Suppressed wrongs seem to now gush through an open spiritual spigot of conscience, and he recalls countless damning judgments that he had made of other people. There are far too many wrongs to remember in detail, but like the prodigal son he cries out for forgiveness.

Although George has only known a form of regimented communal prayer from his schooldays and during his short stint in the army, he feels a compulsion to make a deeply personal and sincere plea for forgiveness. But as he is about to frame the words, he sees himself as a hypocrite pleading for mercy and forgiveness when he showed Buster none. He continues sitting quietly contemplating all these things as if in an isolated capsule suspended in time when he feels someone tapping his shoulder. He turns to see the priest he had met on his first visit.

'You seem to be in deep contemplation.'

George is unwilling to engage in conversation. But the priest sees that George is upset; his watery eyes and his forlorn expression evoke sympathy and pity.

'Aren't you the young man I saw here some months ago?'

George nods.

The priest sits alongside him and points to the corpus on the cross.

'That's not a nice sight, is it? It's like having a statue of a man hanging from the gallows or dying in the electric chair, but that figure tells a different story.'

George doesn't reply.

'What you see in that corpus… that broken body, is sin. Yes, all the sin of the human race wrapped into one sacrificial body.'

George gives the priest a quizzical look and has a flashback memory of discussing sacrifice with Buster on the train.

'Sacrifice is innate to our human nature. To please or placate someone we offer them something of value, something that costs us… even a bunch of flowers that we buy to please a girlfriend can be seen as a form of sacrifice on our part.'

George remains silent.

'But what you see on that cross is a perfect sacrifice… a sacrifice that only God can make on our behalf to free us from sin. No human being on earth can tell us with authority that our sins are forgiven, unless that person is an ordained priest acting *in persona Christi*… or, acting as Christ.'

George is not ready to hear all this and gets up and walks slowly towards the main door of the cathedral when the priest intercepts him, saying, 'Christ had two natures, divine and human, and you, too, have a spiritual dimension.'

The priest beckons him to sit. 'Your soul is restless until it finds peace in God.'

George reflects for a moment before replying, 'I need to find relief from… my guilt.'

'Are you Catholic?'

'No'

The priest puts a hand to George's shoulder. 'Ask the God-Man on the cross to forgive you. Feel His powerful presence in the tabernacle of the holy Eucharist and contemplate the suffering he accepted on our behalf to free us from the slavery of sin. Some crucifixes depict a more accurate image of that reality. Look at the bloodstained, beaten and humiliated figure. That is your sin, my sin and the sin of every human being.'

George listens but makes no reply.

'Do you remember the line from the prayer you may have said at some stage in your life, the *Our Father?* It's all there in that one line, forgive us our trespasses as we forgive those who trespass against us. That's the key phrase.'

George is stung by those words, as he has not even contemplated forgiving Jane, or Buster or Derek, or anyone else who has offended him in the past. He continues gazing at the corpus on the cross. The priest gives him a blessing.

'Find peace in Him… child of God.'

Timeless moments pass and George sees in the battered body of the corpus a reminder of how he had abused his own body in shameful acts, and the crown of thorns symbolically piercing his pride and ego. He is aware of experiencing something intangibly unique in the intense stillness of the cathedral – an abiding sense of consoling grace – something his broken world could never offer. He happens to notice a black man kneeling near the rear and wonders how this church allows him to be there. He is suddenly conscious of the social wrongs that he has committed against people like him and feels a twinge of conscience about the condescending and rude way he sometimes treats his maid Agnes.

A crimson sun is setting in the west as he makes his way along the pavement towards the Alhambra Theatre. He instinctively greets a strange black man, who looks at him askance. He knows he has a long way to go before he can breach the wall of his racial prejudice, but he wants to make a start, and no longer wishes to walk along a path prescribed by a government that is out of touch with social reality and common human decency.

He passes the spot where he had a violent confrontation with Derek, a provoked moment of self-defence that he believes he had handled correctly. But it's a reminder that instant choices will continue to be made that could have good or bad consequences, and it's never a given that he will always choose the right path.

He buys the evening newspaper, dated 11 July 1963, and boards a double-decker trolley bus at the bottom end of Umbilo Road. He climbs to the upper deck where he happens to see Agnes sitting two rows from the back and sits down next to her. The white conductor takes his ticket fare. 'There are plenty of seats up front.' In those days, several seats at the rear of the upper deck were reserved for non-Europeans, as black people were then called. George takes his ticket, looks up at the conductor, 'I'm fine here, thank you.' His deliberate debunking of the normative socio-political protocol receives a disapproving scowl from the conductor. George politely greets Agnes and opens his newspaper to read the headlines that prominent ANC members have been arrested on a smallholding outside Johannesburg while plotting to overthrow the government under the banner of Operation Mayibuye. He shakes his head and turns to the sports page.

The electric power-driven trolley bus glides quietly through the gloomy suburban streets, conveying George to his bus stop from where he takes a short leisurely walk to his new home, not knowing what tomorrow will bring, or what choices he will be compelled to make. But following his cathartic experience in the cathedral, he feels a compulsion to act with gumption; he contacts Charlie to get Jane's address and telephone number knowing that, as an employee of the GPO, he would have access to a Pretoria telephone directory.

'She lives at 142 Klip Street, Muckleneuk,' Charlie informs him, and also gives him the telephone number. 'Be careful, George, she's hurt you once don't be open to another knockout blow. She's not the woman we thought she was.'

George asks his next-door neighbour if Candice could stay over for a few days while he's away in Pretoria. Their young daughter is in Grade One at Penzance Primary School and a new friend of Candice.

On arriving at Jan Smuts Airport, George takes the airport bus to Pretoria and then a taxi to Klip Street, every moment wracking his brain what to say and how to say it. No sooner has he composed one line than it is scrapped in favour of another. He is painfully aware of receiving a final brush-off and to be left further confused and dejected. As the taxi turns into Klip Street, he sees Jane's MG parked in the driveway of number 142. He nervously makes his way to the front door feeling like an automaton with a mechanical message to deliver, even though he can't think which one it will be. Even the small cardboard box he is carrying assumes a weight far beyond its delicate contents. Mrs. Taylor answers the door. She is visibly taken aback. 'Oh, it's you!'

A deathly silence sinks George almost into oblivion.

'Good afternoon, Mrs. Taylor… is it possible to speak with Jane?'

Mrs. Taylor looks more shocked than him standing like an errant fool at the front door asking for the impossible.

'I don't know… I'll check.'

He is now wracked in doubt about the wisdom in coming and wants to toss the box into the nearby bush. Mrs. Taylor returns to say that Jane is not feeling well and thanks him for coming.

'Tell Jane that I'll be across the road in the park,' pointing to Magnolia Dell. 'I'll be there for an hour.'

He is about to turn away when he quickly thrusts the box into her hands. 'Please give her this.'

She closes the door with a look of sadness that connects with his depressed mood.

George finds a grassy spot near the large fishpond and sits there waiting for a miracle. Minutes before the hour he hears a voice behind him.

'Hello, George.'

He spins around to look into the face of the woman he has fallen in love with but who now appears as a stranger. He stands up to reach out to her, but she resists. 'Please… no.'

He stares at a figure of beauty shadowed in remorse. Jane directs him to a bench at the edge of the pond where they sit down. All those many rehearsed lines that had jagged his mind on the plane vanish, all seemingly inadequate and clumsy. They sit in silence absorbing each other's presence. After what seems like a return to a dark age, Jane gently touches his hand, turns to look into his deep brown eyes, and with a voice that has never sounded so placating, says 'Please… if you can… please forgive me.'

He listens to her litany of errors, bad decisions and willful betrayal shaped in words of regret and remorse. 'I was never in love with Derek, but he was exciting to be with and for me, a liberating experience at that stage of my life. He showed life beyond the confines of my strict upbringing. He showed me the physical delights of a world without boundaries… doing what I felt like doing and ignoring the consequences.'

Her words penetrate the protective barrier encapsulating the lonely space into which he has retreated. They winnow in his mind, throwing out the chaff and holding back what sounds good and hopeful.

'So, he sent you to Ladysmith to identify Buster?'

'Yes, and when I saw Buster's broken body and bloodied face, I wanted to get justice for him.'

'How well did you know Buster?'

'We had met a few times together with Derek, but never alone.'

'Did you hate me for what I did to Buster?'

'Initially, yes. I really believed that you had done a terrible thing and that Derek justifiably wanted revenge, but I naively never thought for one moment that it would involve murder.

After the incident outside the Alhambra, he phoned and said he wanted me to get you to the Tropicale Restaurant at Albert Park on a dinner date. He even marked the tree from where he was going to shoot you. When I refused, he was angry and said he would kill you without my help. Then true to his word, he tried to do so when he used an accomplice to shoot you from that passing car.'

George is momentarily silent as he tries to register what she has just told him; he can't get his head around the fact that she had kept all this from him.

'How could you possibly have had any sincere feelings for me, if you were collaborating with that scumbag?'

'I'm sorry George, truly sorry. I'm a coward, I thought if I told you everything, you would hate me, and I didn't want to lose you, because I was falling head over heels in love with you, you idiot.'

She casts her eyes down feeling the weight of her betrayal. 'Little did I realize in my stupidity that by not warning you, I could have lost you in the car shooting incident.' Sobbing gently, she rises from the bench and moves towards the lake. George follows her, pulls her close to him in a deep embrace and whispers in her ear, 'That's all I wanted to hear.'

They walk back in silence to her home. At the door she says in a voice still anchored in regret, 'Thank you for the gift,' and following an awkward pause, adds, 'I couldn't bring myself to open the box but I put my nose to it and I could smell roses.'

Sounding like a gauche teenager, he declares, 'The white rose is your beauty rose and the red one is your love rose, so you never need to forget that... no matter what anyone else tells you.'

They stand in the open doorway looking deeply into each other's eyes, a soul-searching connection that says more than any words could.

'Please come home. Candice misses you terribly.'

'Give me time…' she whispers in almost inaudible syllables.

He kisses her hand, 'Please come back. I love you.'

She closes the front door and he walks towards the gate, giving a cursory glance at the MG that sparks a plethora of mixed memories and emotions. He takes the pavement route into town along Walker Street where he runs his fingers against a row of twin-spiked, green-painted, steel fencing, fearing any new barrier that could keep them apart. Thoughts congest his mind pointing to no clear direction, although he is pleased that she opened her heart to him. But can he truly forgive her? Can he ever trust her again? Without trust, there can be no firm foundation for a stable relationship. Is she not psychologically unstable? To put it crudely, is she damaged goods? He wrestles with these thoughts on the flight back to Durban, looking out of the cabin window across a white foamy sea of puffy clouds, wishing for the plane to float off the curvature of the earth and be lost forever.

The following days are a blur for George as he tries to get back into a daily workday routine. His hardware shop is earning a steady income and he is managing the monthly cash flow. He takes Candice to town on Friday to show her his new enterprise in West Street. His main purpose now is to direct her young life with truth and all the love that he can muster.

This proves to be a really good Friday because on arriving home, Candice goes ahead into the lounge to find Jane sitting on the couch and runs straight into her arms.

'Jane... Jane... '

'Hello, my sweetheart,' and kisses Candice on the cheek.

Flinging her arms around Jane's neck, Candice pleads, 'Please don't ever leave me again.'

George, who is watching from the lounge door, moves to embrace Jane with a loving kiss. He is so overwhelmed that he feels inclined to jump and dance around like a zealous Dervish shouting his head off with joy, but he controls his emotions, saying, 'This calls for a big celebration. Let's all go to the Edward for a delicious Chinese dinner.'

'Oh, yes, daddy, I love Chinese food.'

'And let me drive you there in my sporty MG,' which is parked on the back lawn.

Peter Chen's restaurant is a favourite with George, and the three of them happily embrace its unique setting and Oriental charm. Afterwards, they go for a stroll along the beachfront, where Candice runs a safe distance ahead dancing on her toes in the incoming surf.

'By the way,' George says with forced formality and a winsome smile.

She pauses to listen.

'There's an unanswered proposal I made to you some months ago.'

'Yes, and what about it?' she replies teasingly.

'Well, the offer's still open if you're interested.'

She takes him by the hand and pulls him into the shallows. 'Listen to the waves on the shoreline. They'll tell you the answer.'

'What do you mean? They're just going swishing and swooshing.'

'That's because you don't know how to interpret their language. It's yeshhh... yeshhh... that's what all that whoosing and swooshing is saying.'

Later that evening, Jane phones her parents with the news. Her father asks to speak with George.

'Young man, we are absolutely delighted to welcome you and your lovely daughter, Candice, into our family. I'm on standby to perform the ceremony, should you agree.'

Time moves on apace, and once the invitations have been sent out and the banns called for three consecutive Sundays in the pastor's church, George, Jane and Candice travel to Pretoria for the wedding.

Pretoria, as the administrative capital of the country, exudes a strong middle-European cultural atmosphere fostered by its dominant Afrikaner Calvinist citizenry. It is a period when Afrikaner business enterprises are thriving, and, as an independent republic, the government is trying to forge unity among its white population.

Pretoria, sometimes called Fort Pretoria, because of its burgeoning security forces and laager mentality, stands as a stubborn bulwark against any outside or internal threats. Yet, the outside world is adopting an increasingly critical and hostile view of the country's racial policies, and in August that year, the United Nations Security Council adopts a resolution calling for a voluntary ban on the sale of military equipment to the republic. But this merely spurs the government on to invest in a strong weapons manufacturing industry to overcome this challenge, and to cultivate relations with sympathetic international sources. Most whites feel confident that the government is more than capable of dealing with these external threats, and, on his wedding day, such distracting thoughts are put well aside as George waits to enter the church. He delights in seeing Winnie and Charlie as well as two of his fishing mates from Durban sitting in the pews. He has a reflective thought of his mother, but his heart is thumping with such intense anticipation as he hears the opening chords of Mendelsohn's wedding march, that any further thought of her is lost in the moment. 'This is it!' he says to himself. Standing in front of the bride's father he waits to receive his bride, who enters the church with Candice as one of the flower girls. He feels undeservedly blessed and grateful.

A joyful reception is held at the Culemborg Hotel where happiness is given full spate in lively music, dancing and speeches. George sees Charlie and Winnie waltzing closely and comments, 'Hey, Charlie boy, have you eventually taken the bait?'

Winnie looks lovingly at Charlie, saying, 'I've been trying to snag this old cad, or, should I say shad, for a long time.'

'She's finally pulled you in, Charlie boy.'

'Yup! Hook, line and sinker!'

'Well, that means the end of your love affair with old Chooks.'

'Never! Old Chooks will be extended into a tandem.'

They all laugh joyously. 'And, by the way,' Charlie adds, 'I have been taking driving lessons and have saved up to buy a second-hand car.'

'Well, I can help you there to make a good choice,' replies George with a chuckle.

Winnie puts her arms around Charlie singing, 'Charlie is my darling, my darling, my darling Chevalier…'

'There you have it, Charlie boy, you're a young Chevalier.'

'Forget the age, he's got the stamina of an ox,' retorts Winnie, adding, 'he's my French knight with a Highland bonnet and a big bright claymore to defend me,' she cries aloud, the champagne bubbling merrily in her head.

'A claymore! That's a heavy number,' declares George with a wicked wink.

Winnie's delinquent son, Reggie, is also in a jolly mood and overhears the conversation. 'What's a claymore, mom?'

'It's a Scottish broadsword, my boy,' laughs Charlie, who has a fair knowledge of military equipment, old and modern, 'that teaches young men to be well-behaved, and for wives to be grateful for the love of a man equipped with a heavy-duty weapon.'

With an unsteady hand, Reggie raises an overflowing glass of bubbly to Charlie and Winnie, declaring, 'Let the good times roll!' George wonders how the profligate will be accommodated in the new relationship, but fortunately living so far from his mother he may be only an occasional thorn in the flesh.

George and Jane spend a honeymoon week in the Kruger National Park, observing nature and the wilds in their pristine state, and learning much about animal behaviour. On an early morning game drive they come across a pair of mating lions and are told by the ranger that big cats can mate multiple times a day, sometimes five days in a row, a notion that instinctively feeds into George's passion for his new wife, who is relaxed and no longer expresses moral restraints about enjoying a vibrant sex life. Being so close to these uninhibited spontaneous gestures of creation stimulates their libido, fulfilling a strong mutual desire to extend their family. On the last night, sitting under a spreading acacia tree at the Skukuza bush camp, George is grateful to be given a second chance of a happy marriage and is willing to make changes that would hopefully sustain that dream.

But their happiness is unexpectedly cut short after their return from honeymoon when George receives a visit from Detective Marais, whose stern face instinctively bodes ill tidings.

'Your mother has been found.'

'Was she in Pretoria?'

'She was certainly there at the time of your wedding.'

'Why do you say that?'

'Because she had a picture of you and Jane, presumably cut from the Pretoria News social page of your wedding day. She attached it to…' He pauses briefly out of respect for what he is about to say. 'To her suicide note, which we found on the banks of the river next to some of her personal belongings.'

He hands George the note and the newspaper wedding picture. Tears well up in his eyes as he reads the report.

'The body of an unidentified white female was found at Hennops River, near the popular picnic spot.'

He lets the newspaper clipping slip from his hand as if it doesn't exist. Marais picks it up, saying, 'There's something else you should read.'

A one-line message scribbled in her inimitable handwriting cuts deep into his heart. 'My dear loving son, George, please forgive me.'

Marais politely doffs hat in respect and leaves.

Jane comes to the front door and stands next to George sensing that something awful has been communicated to him. He passes her the note and the newspaper clipping. 'It says she drowned in the Hennops River. Cause of death, suicide!' Jane shakes her head in disbelief.

They close the door and share the sad news with Candice.

'Has Granny gone to heaven?'

'We have a merciful God, Candice,' Jane says sweetly.

Candice runs to her room crying bitterly for a gran who doted and showered deep affection on her. George looks sadly at Jane as he reads the date of the note. 'She chose her birthday to do it.'

Jane puts a comforting arm around him.

George is called back to Pretoria to formally identify the body. He gives his mother a dignified funeral from Rogers Funeral Parlour in Church Street West and buys a burial plot at the Rebecca Street Cemetery but refuses to erect a tombstone.

Shortly after his return to Durban, he visits his lawyer who now has a death certificate to tie up the property rights of the maisonette, which pass to him. Winnie is to receive all her personal belongings, including her jewellery, while George inherits her small investment account, with the proviso that he makes provision for Candice's education.

A suburban complacency sets in as George and Jane build

a new life together. She is using her bookkeeping background to assist him in the business and Candice is looking forward to Grade One the following year.

But the human spirit that seeks a permanent, peaceful existence has to be completely honest, and George knows that he is still living a lie. Although he laid his sins at the foot of the cross in the cathedral and asked forgiveness, he has yet to make reparation for two extremely serious offences; premeditated murder and lying under oath. So far, he has managed to get off scot-free.

George, however, is fully preoccupied with more immediate and exciting plans to build a secure, suburban castle for Queen Jane and Princess Candice. At the beginning of his second marriage, he is committed to making it work by sacrificing time and energy to the two most important people in his life, yet still unable to suppress the guilt that he carries. Psychologically, the weight of this guilt weighs heavily upon his mind and he is often over-anxious to lock out the outside world. So, like any king of a castle, he pulls up the drawbridge at night to keep out those who could harm its occupants. But his castle has no towers or thick walls and although it is built on firm foundations, it is still sitting on a bed of sand leaving open his interior to the soul-searching forces of heaven.

Acknowledgements

Sandra Herrington
Special thanks to my wife, Sandra, for her valuable advice and input as editor.

Deirdre Harris and Johann van den Berg
Additional gratitude to Deirdre Harris and former Dean of Science at the University of KwaZulu-Natal, Johann van den Berg, for their incisive comments and proof reading.

Clive Thompson
To Clive Thompson for his highly creative and excellent layout and cover design of the book.

Deirdre Harris
Front and back cover paintings by Cape Town artist, Deirdre Harris.

Google
And finally, to Google as a research platform for dates, events and people.

Other Books by the Author

Growing Old in 'Black" South Africa is a sequel to Neville Herrington's successful earlier book **Growing Up in 'White' South Africa,** and is a continuation of his life's journey against the backdrop of a changing socio-political and, at times, turbulent landscape as the country transitioned from nearly half a century of enforced racial segregation to the inclusive democratic society it is today.

A romping journey through the adventures of post-war youth searching for self-identity in a rapidly changing world. The author captures the sounds, smells, nuances, events and special characteristics of a period that remains etched in his memory which should resonate with those who lived through it and fascinate those that didn't.

The Brigid O'Meara Trilogy

In a riveting story laced with romance, humour, political intrigue and violence against the backdrop of the infamous Jameson Raid that triggered the Anglo-Boer War, Brigid O'Meara, a beautiful Irish musical hall performer finds herself drawn into the intrigues of a group of British Uitlander sympathisers, who are planning the overthrow of Paul Kruger's Boer Republic.

In this sequel, Brigid, as an Irish nationalist, is drawn into the conflict of the Anglo Boer War by identifying with and entering into the struggle of the Boers to retain their independence. Her loyalty to the Boer cause leads to her incarceration in a British concentration camp and separation from a British Uitlander, accused of high treason, with whom she is romantically involved.

In the aftermath of the war, Brigid becomes an unwitting host of a demonic entity that plunges her into a dark world of evil and depravity from which she ultimately triumphs. It is a world that alienates her from those she loves and one that brings into focus the hypocritical social morals and sanctimonious self-righteousness of the new ruling British colonials.

ELSIE is the story of a young woman caught up in the turmoil of World War 1 and her courageous efforts to bring sanity to her broken world. The reader is taken back to December 1916, when thousands of South African soldiers are returning home after serving in German East Africa. The world they return to is a changed one, with many having no job and finding alternative opportunities in criminal activity. Alarmed at seeing a world implode with the escalating violence on the European warfront, she determines to play her part by volunteering as a nurse at a military hospital on the Western Front where she is exposed to the horrors of industrial warfare, and is forced to confront the futility of it all.

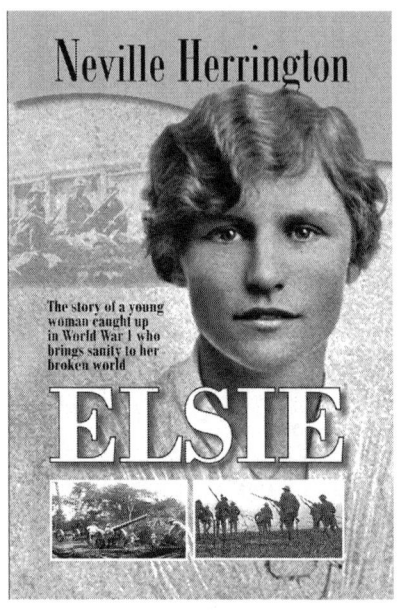

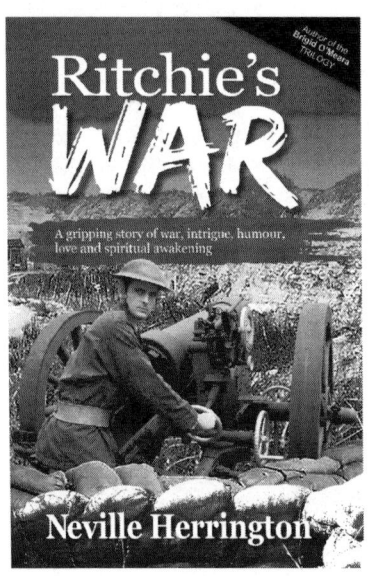

RITCHIE'S WAR is a gripping story of war, intrigue, humour, love and spiritual awakening. The year is 1916, and at age 19 Ritchie is launched into a world conflict that he doesn't fully comprehend. It is a time when the opposing sides in World War I are European countries that have drawn on their colonies to assist in their continental dispute. Ritchie volunteers for service in East Africa, and, although excited by the prospects of a great adventure, soon begins to feel like a pawn in a game of chess that is being manipulated by external forces to their own advantage

Contact:
Sandy Herrington
Phone: 031 261 1034
email: sandyh@iafrica.com
web: www.tekweni.co.za